I GOT YOUR *Back*

Teflon & Tatiana's Love Story

A NOVEL BY

SHVONNE LATRICE

© 2020
Published by First Class
Publishing Group
www.theshvoneelatrice.com

ALL RIGHTS RESERVED

Contains explicit language & adult themes suitable for ages 16+

$18.99
ISBN 978-1-966375-21-0

CHAPTER ONE

Tatiana Drew

"Guess who's in the house ladies? Breviinnnnn!" the club's deejay shouted loudly as hell as Brevin and I were escorted up into the VIP section.

"Why does he have to announce you to the women only, Brevin?" I whispered into my boyfriend's ear as we sat down on the velvet plush couches. I didn't know why I hadn't become used to this shit by now.

"Chill Tati, damn," he scoffed and shook his head as if I were beyond annoying to him.

Blowing out hot air, I leaned back and closed my eyes while rubbing my stomach. I was currently four months pregnant, but for some reason I felt fat and sick all the damn time. My stomach wasn't even bulging really, but I ate like a horse and felt like a cow. It was quite obvious that something was going on in my midsection though because of my small stature.

"You need a drink, boo?" Some waitress walked into the VIP area holding a big ass bottle of Grey Goose, while smiling down at Brevin.

"Of course." He nodded, biting his lip and eyeing her body.

Brevin and I had been together for three years now and at first, it was perfect. So perfect that I gave him, my virginity that I'd been saving for twenty-two years. I thought I'd found the ideal fairytale relationship, but after only a year, that feeling had completely vanished.

Brevin ran Cleveland, by moving weight throughout Ohio. Because of that, he made a lot of money too and with money came women, power, and anything else that could be bought. I knew he was cheating on me, but I didn't have much proof these days; it was just a feeling, which was strong as hell. It was all my intuition I guess you could say. He stayed out all night, he never let me see his phone, and there have been multiple occasions where a bitch has run up on us going ape shit. Of course, he pretended like she was some random groupie every damn time.

Contrary to popular belief, women don't just act out for no reason at all. They've gotten attention somewhere at some point. It may have been months ago, even years, but no woman goes insane based off simple eye contact; that's more of a man thing.

I wanted to leave Brevin and had planned to but that was before I found out I was pregnant again; I lost our first child. When I told Brevin, he promised he would be different and that we wouldn't have any more problems, but I wasn't so sure about that anymore. Because here I was almost five months pregnant, and he was eye fucking the VIP hostess in my face. To say I was miserable in my relationship would be an understatement.

"Can I have some apple juice please," I said, snapping her from the staring contest she was having with Brevin.

"Sure." She turned on her heels and switched, as he watched, not even caring that I was right here next to him.

"I don't even want to be here anymore." I shook my head and looked off.

"Why?" he frowned.

"I saw you looking at her, Brevin! I swear I'm so tired of this shit. You promised things would be different but it's still looking the same!" My eyes began to water. These damn hormones had me acting a fool.

"Tati, baby I was just looking. I love you baby, but that doesn't mean I'm blind now. She's an attractive woman, but she ain't you. You and the baby are all I care about, not these hood rats." He lightly kissed the area next to my nose, stopping a tear that was on its way down. "Aight?"

"Yeah," I whispered, not believing a word he'd said, but angry that my heart didn't yearn for him any less.

I bobbed my head to the music as I watched Brevin's best friend Mack walk up into the VIP area with his girlfriend Gloria. Brevin and Mack had attempted to make us become friends but it just didn't work out because we were nothing alike. She was a stripper who liked to do dirty shit on the low and behind her man's back, while I was just trying to live normally; well as normal as I could being in a relationship with a big time drug dealer like Brevin Williamson.

"Hey," she waved and threw her long weave behind her shoulder. "When is the baby due?" she sat down next to me, slapping me in the face with whatever perfume she was wearing.

"September." I smiled.

"What's good, Tati?" Mack leaned down to hug me, before sitting back down next to Brevin. They began whispering and laughing about something, and I knew it meant that they had plans to be up to no good.

"Them niggas make me sick." Gloria sucked her teeth.

"Why do you say that?"

"Come on Tatiana, you know what they're whispering about. They're figuring out how to ditch us so they can go lay up with some bitches."

I was going to respond but I decided not to because I had nothing to say. Well I had plenty to say but I didn't want to let it out. I agreed with Gloria, but I didn't want to give her the satisfaction of being right about *my* man. Also I didn't want to believe what I already knew to be true.

However, sitting here thinking was making me sick to my stomach, and I didn't want to be in this atmosphere anymore. Lately anything that had to do with Brevin and his kingpin lifestyle disgusted me.

"Brev, I'm gonna go home." I stood to my feet and smoothed my dress down. He stared up at me as I tousled my short curly hair from one side to the other.

"Baby why? Shit is just getting started?" I could see a frown forming on his handsome face.

"The baby and I just don't feel good."

He chuckled and rose to his feet, towering over me. Brevin stood at about 6'3, had smooth light skin, curly hair, and a perfectly trimmed goatee. He was a beautiful man to say the least, with smarts, money, and the city of Cleveland in his hands. That's how everyone from the outside looking in saw him, but I knew the real Brevin. He was insecure, a cheater, a liar, controlling, and he could get abusive if things didn't go his way. It may sound cliché, but I was with him because of the baby and only because of the baby. As I said earlier, my bags were packed when I found out I was pregnant. Love was barely enough anymore.

"Sit yo' ass down, Tati," he gritted in my ear, gripping my small bicep in his huge hand.

"Brevin—"

"You wanna make a fucking scene in here shorty? Huh? I already let you slide earlier but if you keep it up I can embarrass you."

Blinking away the tears in my eyes, I slowly slid my arm from his grasp and sat my ass back down. Gloria had her eyebrows raised so high they were damn near touching her hairline. Brevin straightened his Gucci suit just as a few women came into the VIP dancing to "Worst Behavior" by Drake. I just sat there, in a trance, wondering how my life had come to this, and before I knew it, it was time to leave. Thank you, Jesus.

Brevin's driver dropped us off at our home in Ohio City, and I was just hoping to take a bath and go to bed. I was exhausted, mentally and didn't feel like talking, touching, or anything. I wanted to be alone honestly.

"I'm sorry about earlier." Brevin plopped down onto the bed as I began to remove my dress. I just stared in the mirror, ignoring him. He was about to give the same speech he always gave when he got rough with me. "I just don't like when you don't do what I tell you, Tatiana. I love you and I wanna be better, but you make it hard for me to do so."

Once I was undressed, I grabbed my robe and walked towards the bathroom in our room. Before I could make it past him good, he grabbed me and laid me down on the bed. Pulling my robe open, he looked over my body before kissing on my neck sloppily. His lips felt disgusting, not warm, sensual, and soft like usual.

"Brevin, stop," I whispered as he dropped his head between my legs, kissing my lower lips through my panties.

"Relax, Tati."

I blew out hot air as he tugged my panties down my legs. They barely made it off before he was sucking on my clit and massaging my legs. Tucking my bottom lip into my mouth, I pressed my head back into the bed and gripped the sheets in my hands. Brevin's sex game was undeniably perfect. I didn't know which was better, his dick or his mouth.

"Brevin, baby," I whimpered as I massaged his soft curly hair.

My body quivered and jerked lightly as he let his tongue run amuck all over my clit. My body released and he lapped up all of my juices as if he were thirsty for it this whole time. Removing his head from between my legs, he licked his sexy lips and then smiled at me as I struggled to catch my breath.

"We cool?" he raised a brow and I just nodded. He walked to the bathroom, brushed his teeth, and then grabbed his ringing phone from the dresser. "I will be back in a little bit. Some shit went down," he lied. I knew him.

"Like what?"

"Trap got robbed." He shrugged one shoulder.

"Shouldn't you have people under you that can handle that, Brevin?"

I was asking something I already knew the answer to. I wasn't that girlfriend who was completely oblivious to what her man did. I'd eavesdropped on more conversations than I could count. I knew everything about his empire… he just didn't know that.

"Remember your place, Tatiana. When I need your help, you will know. Don't wait up." He gripped the doorknob and left before I could respond.

I refused to believe this was as far as my life would go.

I Got Your Back ◆ *Teflon & Tatiana's Love Story*

CHAPTER ONE

Brevin Williamson

As soon as I climbed in my Wraith, I lit a blunt and took a big ass pull. Tonight I just wanted to have fun, but Tatiana always had to ruin some shit. All I wanted to do was party with my people, but she had to get upset because I was looking at other women.

I ain't fucking blind and to be honest she knows the damn deal. I'm a muthafucking kingpin, how can she expect me to be with her and only her when women were everywhere? I can't do shit without a bitch trying to suck me up or let me fuck. She needs to be mad at these bitches, not me, because it's not like I go out looking. I haven't had to work for pussy in years and I liked it that way.

As I got high as a muthafucka in my driveway, my phone began ringing again. I looked down at it to see it was my boy Mack, prompting a smile to spread across my face. I knew he had some bitches because in a way that was his job. When I couldn't scope because of Tatiana, he knew he had to do it for me. And it ain't like he didn't get to test the pussy too. I always threw him the hoes I didn't want, or the ones I'd already fucked. A nigga like Mack who was never able to get bitches back in the day didn't mind getting thrown scraps. I was even fucking his main bitch Gloria, and he wasn't gonna do shit about it. He knew the game and he knew I reigned supreme out here. Stepping to me about busting down his bitch would get his head blown open, best friend or not.

"What's good, patna?" I smiled before taking another pull. I caught a glimpse of my reflection in my side mirror making me grin. I was a handsome ass nigga and every chick in Ohio knew that.

"Aye, come through. We at Groove's crib and he got all the girls there."

"I thought we were supposed to chill at your crib?" I frowned, blowing out smoke.

"We were, but Gloria is at the house and I don't wanna hear her mouth."

His response made me suck my teeth because that hoe had her nerve. I was beating that pussy up almost as much as Tatiana's and she had the nerve to be clocking how many bitches Mack fucked. And he was just as dumb for letting her do so. Ain't no way I'd be claiming a girl getting fucked by my homie. I wish a nigga of mine would step to Tatiana; he'd get bludgeoned in a hot second.

"Hoe got her nerve bro. You need to stop acting like a bitch. You pay the bills up in that muthafucka. Move the party to your crib; I ain't driving all the way to Saint Clair."

"Man aight."

We disconnected and I finished off my blunt before speeding to Mack's home. I'd obviously gotten there before him, because I didn't see his car in the driveway, so I just rang the doorbell. Gloria answered, smiling widely than a muthafucka as I pushed her backward lightly. We made our way to the bathroom, and as soon as I closed the door, she was on her knees.

"Hurry up because some people are coming," I bit down on my lip as she unbuckled my slacks.

She had my dick out in no time and was slobbering all over my shit. I hit the back of my head on the door as she continued to move her lethal ass mouth up and down my shaft. Palming the back of her head, I made her move faster as I humped her face. She only gagged a little bit, but that shit had me ready to nut immediately. Gloria's head game was one to be reckoned with, and I was surprised she wasn't out here charging for it. Maybe she was, but she wasn't ringing me up for a got damn thing.

"Shit, Gloria, fuck!" I groaned, fucking her face feverishly. "Ahhhh! Shit!" I called out in a high-pitched voice as I spilled my seeds down her throat.

She swallowed it up and flashed her pretty smile, just as we heard a bunch of rowdy niggas coming into the house.

"I don't even suck his dick like that." She pointed, referring to Mack.

"Too bad for him." I shrugged, fixing myself.

"You're always fucking me and I'm always fucking you, so why don't we just be together, Brevin? You obviously don't love Tatiana and I damn sure don't love Mack. I'm only with him because I get to see you and he pays my way."

"I do love Tatiana. It's just she's pregnant right now and the last time she miscarried it was shortly after we had sex."

"Well hopefully I will have your baby and not her," she mumbled.

"Fuck is that supposed to mean?" I grimaced. Her angry expression immediately softened upon seeing mine.

"Nothing Brevin, I just—"

WHAM!

I backhanded her ass so hard she spun like a ballerina and fell backwards into the bathtub. Her nose was busted, and I really didn't give a fuck. Her hoping Tatiana lost the baby had hit a fucking nerve. I may not have been a sympathetic nigga, but I wanted my kid.

"Watch yo' mouth. And from now on this shit is done."

I left out of the bathroom not caring who saw her sitting in the bathtub with a fucked up nose. When I got into the living room, my homies Mook, Tone, and Groove were sitting on the couch as Mack popped open some bottles. Mack was looking at me uncomfortably, and I knew it was about his bitch. He knew not to make a peep about the shit though.

As I sat down, the doorbell rang so Mook got up to answer it. About eight fine ass bitches walked in smiling and saying hi. I didn't know who I wanted, but all my homies knew I got first pick. I didn't mind if they fucked after though.

Groove was the only one I would allow to pick his own bitch, but he rarely dabbled since he was trying to be faithful to his sexy ass baby mama. I'd fuck that in a minute.

POP! POP! POP! POP! POP!

After the last girl came in, some nigga started letting off shots. Everyone began scrambling and screaming, while trying to duck for cover. After an hour of fucking shooting it seemed, the bullets finally stopped flying everywhere and breaking shit.

"Brevin stay away from my bitch!" the shooter hollered, as I stayed ducked behind the couch. "And stay away from my territory!"

I waited for a little bit, before finally standing up. Five of the girls were dead, right along with my niggas Mook and Tone. Running my hands over my face, I punched the wall, making a big ass hole in it.

"What the fuck!" I shouted, feeling a vibration in my chest as the three living girls cried and screamed over their dead friends.

"Nigga, whose bitch did you fuck?" Groove frowned at me.

"Hell if I know! Close the fucking door!" I barked at Mack. "Call someone to come clean these fucking bodies up man. I'm going to the back; I can't leave out right now." I said before exiting the room so they could handle that shit.

Entering Mack's guest room, I plopped down on the bed and removed my shoes and jacket. Lying flat, I closed my eyes wondering what I was gonna do now that I didn't have Mook and Tone. As I laid there in the dark, pondering, the door opened and I saw Gloria walking in.

"I'm sorry," she whispered, closing it behind her.

"Me too shorty, come here," I replied, feeling a bulge appear in my slacks.

She walked her sexy ass over, undressed, and then got into the bed with me. While Mack cleaned up my mess, I was about to fuck his bitch.

CHAPTER ONE

Tre Wayne "Teflon" German

Los Angeles, California...

Say my life is like a movie nigga, fucking every day, fucking every day, nigga fucking every day. Say my life is like a movie nigga, fucking every day, fucking every day, nigga fucking every day. Missionary, doggy-style, nigga fucking every way.

A big ass grin covered my face as I watched this thick ass girl shake her ass in my face. Her along with three other bitches were doing the most right now to get some of these bills my homie Merce and I had clutched in our hands. I had every intention on spending every single dollar I brought into this club because I could and therefore I would.

See a nigga had a little obsession with the strippers; it was healthy though, in my opinion. I didn't come in here on the daily dropping thirty thousand dollars, but when I came I showed the fuck out.

"Whoever invented strip clubs is a damn genius." Merce stared at one of the girls popping her ass in his lap as he sipped his drink.

"Who the fuck you telling, nigga? I'm ready to move into this muthafucka. I wanted a pole in my crib but Kayla wasn't having that shit."

"Who was gon' be on the pole? I know not her ass."

"Hell nah," I scoffed, thinking about my girlfriend Kayla.

Kayla was beautiful, smart, loyal, and everything us niggas claimed we wanted in a female, but she wasn't enough. I know you're thinking I'm a shady ass nigga, and I couldn't agree more. Kayla was every nigga's dream, except mine. I loved her like a fat kid loved cake, but I loved all women. By saying that, it was hard for me to fuck with one woman… sexually. However, Kayla was the only one I was spending my money on, and she was the only woman I was claiming. Shit, I was only eating *her* pussy, but as far as the dick, I was giving a little bit of that to more than a few females. I couldn't help the shit.

I'm twenty-eight, old enough to have matured and have my wild oats sewed, but honestly that hadn't happened yet. I wish I could be the way Kayla wanted me to be, but I just… couldn't.

My African American father and Vietnamese mother raised me, and my dad pretty much did whatever he wanted and when he wanted. He was a great father in the sense that he provided for us, loved us, and spent time with his family like he should have. My dad's only problem was keeping his dick in his pants. I'm sure I had some half siblings floating around out there; I just had to.

My mother, Tam, was still alive and well, living over in Cleveland,

Ohio. As for my dad, Tracy, he just fell off the face of the earth. He left one day to go to a bar when I was fourteen, and he just never came back. Over a decade has gone by, and no one has seen or heard from him. My mom opened a missing person's case, but eventually that shit went cold. I felt in my heart he was dead, but my mom didn't like me to think that way. It's crazy that despite how badly he treated her, she still loved him.

Unfortunately for me though, my father passed his problem right down to me and my older brother Torrey. My little brother Thomas was a good dude, a square almost, but he was better than we were in more ways than one. My mother swears that Torrey and I can be different and when we find the one we will see, but that shit just doesn't seem to be true.

As far as my brothers, Torrey has been locked up for five years for attempted murder, but will be back on the streets in about eleven months. He beat his baby mama Audrina's ass until she was unconscious; we thought she was dead. You'd think she'd be done with that nigga but nope, she'd been holding him down back in my hometown of Cleveland, Ohio, and was actually happy that he'd be out soon. Torrey had always been a troublemaker though, ever since he was eleven and I was eight. For as long as I've known him he's been a fuck up.

Thomas, my baby brother, he was currently a sophomore at Cleveland State University, working to get a degree in business. He had a girlfriend that he loved more than anything and treated like a queen. Although Thomas was my younger brother, I low-key admired the life he led. Like right now, he was studying abroad in Paris. I swear he got all the good genes, and Torrey and I got the fucked up ones.

"What are you doing later?" the stripper in front of me smiled. She was thick as fuck, had pretty brown skin, and some lips that I knew could suck the shit out of my dick. I would be finding out too.

"You." I half smiled and she giggled and shit.

"I can't wait. Let me go get my stuff." She winked and left out of our section. I watched her fat ass the whole way until she disappeared, just imagining hitting that shit from the back. Damn. I ran my hand over my face at my thoughts.

"I'll be right back." Merce stood to his feet as the girl who was dancing in his lap prior pulled on his hand to follow her. "I'm just gon' get some top before I go home. I ain't trying to be bothered the whole night," he added under a low tone and I just nodded while laughing.

As I was waiting for old girl to come back so we could leave, I made eye contact with another stripper who was even sexier than she was.

"You wanna come too?" I raised a brow, watching her nibble on the corner of her lip seductively. She shook her head 'yes' and came to sit in my lap to wait.

"What's your name?"

"Janet, that's my real name."

"I figured." I half smiled.

My phone buzzed, and I looked down to see it was Kayla so I hit ignore. I already knew she was about to question me and ask me if I was coming home when she knew the answer already. If I were coming home, I would've been there by 9pm, that's how it always was. If I wasn't there by that time I was staying out all night.

Sighing dejectedly, I was about to put my phone up until it started ringing again. I looked down to see it was this shorty named Promise who I fucked with on occasions. I hit ignore on her ass too because she seemed to think that she had the same privileges as Kayla and stayed trying to question me. I laughed at the thought.

"Ready," the initial stripper came out.

"Cool, umm Janet is gonna come too. I forgot your name though," I spoke honestly.

She told me but that shit slipped my mind. And since I wasn't one to hold my tongue, it wasn't shit for me to come right out and ask her what it was. If she was salty, she could take her ass home alone.

"Eva," she rolled her eyes subtly. Subtly enough for me to still be interested in seeing what the pussy was like. I hated females with attitude problems, which was another reason Kayla and I clashed.

We left the club and I drove them to the Springhill Suites in El Segundo. It was a pretty nice hotel, but it wasn't too nice if you know what I mean. I was here to fuck and nothing more. I had no plans on wining and dining anybody tonight. And my crib was not a fucking option, not only because Kayla was there, but because I didn't bring random hoes home.

Grabbing my phone, I cut some music on and both ladies began to sway sensually while removing their clothes. Propping myself up on my elbows on the bed, I leaned back to watch them in awe. Once they were both naked, they made their way over to me, helping me remove my clothes. Eva tried to kiss my lips but I blocked her ass with the quickness. I didn't kiss anybody but my girl, and that shit wasn't changing any time soon.

Janet got down on her knees and took my dick into her mouth, sucking on the tip, and that shit was to fucking die for. I swear she had so much damn saliva in her mouth, that I wouldn't be surprised if I busted early. Gripping her hair tightly, I guided her up and down my dick, fucking her face as Eva got down to help her out. Watching two sexy ass females give me some top was the business. Feeling like I was about to nut, I pulled out and let loose on Janet's face, smiling as I did it.

"Clean up and come back," I told her. Janet nodded and got up to clean herself, while I bent Eva over on the bed. I rolled the condom down, and then slipped inside of her, moving slowly at first as she whimpered and moaned loudly. "Shit!" I grumbled.

"Tef, shit, uuuh!" she yelled as I began to beat it up. Seeing her ass move all about had my dick getting harder and harder by the damn second. "Oh my gosh! Oh!" she screamed as she let her juices go.

Janet came back just in time, so I switched the condom and laid down on my back. Mounting me, she slowly pushed herself down, and damn her pussy was tight and wet. Eva's was good too, but I was happy I'd saved Janet's sexy ass for last. As she rode me with precision, Eva licked and sucked on Janet's nipples, turning me on.

"Ahhhh, ahhh uhh!" Janet yowled as she exploded. I was right behind her, filling the condom up. Plopping down on my chest, she panted, attempting to catch her breath.

The three of us laid there for a minute, before going for another round, and knocking the fuck out. I woke up at around 2am though and sent their asses' home in an Uber. I liked having the bed to myself.

CHAPTER ONE

Tatiana

Back in Cleveland, Ohio...

"Eddie wants to know if you're up to helping with the next event?" my co-worker and best friend Jadynn asked as she sat down at my kitchen table.

Jadynn and I met in middle school, and somehow through high school and college, we managed to stay as close as ever. I know people say you outgrow others as you mature, but that never happened with Jadynn. She and I were like Thelma and Louise. She had my back like nobody else, and I had hers the same. We'd gone through all kinds of shit together from putting sugar in niggas' tanks, to fighting bitches who didn't come correct. I mean I'd only been with Brevin, so most of the sugar pouring was on her nigga's cars, but you get the point.

"Tell him yes and yes again if you have to. Why does he keep sending you to ask me when he can call me himself?" I smiled as I brought the tray containing two chicken salads and two glasses of iced tea.

"That's what I told him, but he claims he may offend you if he asks as a man. But I will tell him that it's a go."

"Who is the party for?"

"A football player who just got signed; he wants to throw this big bash at Mellow Nightclub. You, Everly, and I are in charge of the whole damn event. Eddie said the club owner is counting on us to make sure everyone is there and that everyone has a good time."

"Don't we always?"

"Yes but this is the club's first celebrity event so I think the owner is just a little paranoid." She ate some of her salad.

"Well he should know he's with the best."

Jadynn and I both did PR for our boss Eddie's public relations firm. We mainly worked with restaurants, club venues, bars, and things like that, making sure any time someone visited Cleveland they were stopping by one of our clients' places. This event in particular was being hosted at one of our client's clubs, so we had to make sure that everything turned out perfectly. We wanted to make it so that the people who attended, and this newly signed football player, not only became regulars, but also spread the word to other people. There was no promotion like word of mouth.

Jadynn and I were paid pretty well, especially when the event was big news or the client had a lot of money. We were both doing well to only be twenty-five.

"He will see that once the event is over. So how did last night go?"

She raised a brow before sipping her iced tea.

"It went the same way all of his fucking parties go. I wish you would have come, I only had Gloria there."

"Gloria, ugh. And I didn't come because I don't like his parties or his thirsty ass friends who think just because they roll with him they can fuck me."

"I know, I know. It just would have been nice to have some company in the midst of it all."

Just as I finished my sentence, Brevin came in looking like he'd had a wild night. I knew damn well that when he left it wasn't to handle business, and it was evident by the lipstick stains on his crotch that he'd attempted to wipe off. Jadynn saw the shit too, because she made eye contact with me and shook her head.

"What's up, Jadynn?" He nodded his head up and scratched his curly hair.

"Hey, Brevin." She waved lazily.

"Baby." He leaned down to kiss my face and I wanted to move but I also didn't want to upset his crazy ass. "How's the baby?" he touched my stomach and I slightly recoiled.

"It's fine, Brevin. Go clean yourself up." I nudged him off.

Both Jadynn and I watched him leave before we both made eye contact.

"I'm not gonna say too much because it'll be the pot calling the kettle black, but I can't stand his ass Tati. And look at that bruise on your arm."

"Russell ain't no better."

"He's not, but at least he knows how to keep his hands to himself. Look I know my nigga ain't shit and I shouldn't be talking, but I just don't want him to hurt you or the child. You were so sad when you lost the last one—"

"Jadynn, I know. I get it. Brevin gets rough sometimes but he's not gonna do anything to make me lose the baby. He wants it just as badly as I do."

"Yes but accidents happen and I don't want an accident happening to you."

"It won't." I half smiled and she nodded. Brevin was psycho, but he was just as sad as I was when I lost the last baby, so he would never do anything to jeopardize this one. I knew it. I knew him.

Jadynn and I finished our lunch, talked a little bit, and then she went home. I was a bit tired so I decided to head upstairs and take a nap. However, I couldn't even fall asleep really because all I saw were those lipstick stains on Brevin's crotch. I loved him and I wanted us to be a family, but I wasn't sure how much longer I could last with him acting the way he did. I wasn't going to threaten my health by sleeping with a man who sleeps with all of Ohio. All of this was so confusing and I was just beyond conflicted. I felt like God had something better for me, but then again maybe this really was it.

"Sorry about that baby, business went on longer than expected," Brevin walked into the bedroom, prompting me to sit up.

"There was lipstick on your pants, Brevin."

"What? Nah Mack, Groove, and I went to have a burger and I

guess some of the ketchup got onto my pants ma, damn!"

"Damn? The hell do you mean *damn?*" I got off the bed, I was angry now. "Nigga I should be the only one mad! You're coming up in here at twelve in the damn afternoon with another bitch's lipstick on your pants and you're the one mad? Nigga, I should slap the shit out of you!" I shoved his tall muscular ass, but he didn't go anywhere. I wasn't even half of his size.

"Back yo' little ass up!" he wrapped his hand around my neck, but not too tightly because I could still breathe. "I told you it was ketchup and that's the end of it." He tossed me onto the bed.

I couldn't help it so I began to sob lightly. I was trying to be happy because I had a baby coming and a man that most bitches dreamed of being with, but it was hard to keep lying to myself. I couldn't remember the last time I was genuinely happy in my relationship. The only time I smiled was when I was away from home, out with Jadynn, or at work.

"Tati, baby I'm sorry. I didn't mean to grab you like that. I'm just stressing because I got shot at last night." He knelt down in front of me.

Lifting my head from my hands I asked, "You did?"

"Yeah, I did. You know Mook and Tone?" I nodded in response. "They got killed. My homies are dead, and you know they were my shooters."

"I'm sorry baby," I sniffled. "What are you gonna do now?"

"I have to find some new people to be on my team, but I can't deal with no amateurs you know?" He sat next to me, so I leaned my head on his shoulder. Draping his arm around me, he began rubbing up and down my bicep before kissing my forehead. "I'm stressing right now, so forgive me for being rough, okay?"

"Okay."

He kissed me softly while rubbing the small bulge in my stomach. I just caressed the side of his face as our tongues became entangled with one another.

"I love you Tati and I promise shit ain't gonna always be like this."

CHAPTER TWO

Jadynn Davidsen

After eating and chilling with Tatiana, I was feeling tired as hell. I wanted to take advantage of my day off because with this big ass event for Mellow coming up, I would be working nonstop. I didn't mind when I saw my paychecks though. Nope, not at all.

Pulling into the parking structure of my apartment in Downtown, I quickly shut off the engine and grabbed the Tupperware that Tatiana gave me. I loved her chicken salads, so she made sure to make a whole lot so I could take some home.

Looking at the salad made me think about her situation. Yeah, I had a weak ass nigga that I couldn't let go, but my man didn't hit me. Tatiana was little, I mean so was I, but she was smaller than I was and Brevin was huge. He was over six feet and muscular as fuck, and I didn't like that he manhandled her like they were the same damn size. I wouldn't be able to forgive myself if something happened to her, so I just had to say something when I could. I prayed that she got away and soon.

"Hey," I walked into my apartment to see my boyfriend Russell pulling a beer from the fridge.

"Sup shorty, when are you going grocery shopping?" he had the nerve to ask me.

"I planned on going tomorrow. I go every Saturday Russell; you know that. And we should have some food in there." I frowned at his ass.

Russell was only good for eating pussy and fucking. He had jobs here and there but the nigga could never keep them. Every time I looked up his ass was getting fired and claiming that it was the manager's fault and not his. The only reason I was with him was because I was lazy.

See I met him when I was twenty-three and we'd been together ever since then. I put a lot into my relationship with him; I was used to him and comfortable. I knew there were much better niggas out there, but I didn't feel like going out, getting to know someone, and all that bullshit. I was content, so why go looking for something new.

"You cooking?" He cracked the beer open.

"Dinner yes, but I just ate lunch with Tatiana already."

"Damn, do you ever have time for a nigga? All you do is go chill with Tatiana and work? Where do I fucking fit in? I'm your man!"

"Oh my gosh," I sighed.

"You damn right oh my gosh! I wouldn't be surprised if you were eating her damn pussy all the damn time y'all spend together."

"And on that note, I will be in the back taking a nap."

"I'll be back some time later then."

"Where are you going? I swear I'm gonna change the locks on your ass, that will teach you to stop staying out all night for no reason!"

"You don't worry about where the fuck I'm going, Jadynn. When you learn to make time for a nigga, maybe then I will answer yo' fucking questions!" he barked before leaving.

As soon as he left, I went to my bedroom and dialed AT&T. As the line trilled, I began gathering my stuff to take a hot shower since I was in for the rest of the day. The representative finally answered, and after verifying the necessary information, she asked me what I needed help with.

"Yes, I'd like to cut one of the lines off please."

"Okay, which one would that be?" she asked.

"The one ending in 3112."

This nigga had me fucked up. I was not in the business of raising a man and since he'd rather stay out all night instead of hitting the computer keys to apply for some jobs, I was gonna start cutting him off slowly; monetary wise. I was tired of buying him phones, clothes, shoes, and other material things.

"There is a disconnection fee since you're in the middle of the contract Ms. Davidsen. Is that alright?"

"That's fine." The money would be well worth it. If he had any hoes, he'd better hope they could get his ass a phone because this one was no longer.

"You're all set!"

"Great, thank you." I hung up the phone and proceeded to take my shower and lie down.

A few hours later…

"Hey, hey," someone shook me. I opened my eyes to see my sister Paige staring down into my face.

"What time is it?" I sat up, pushing my auburn colored hair behind my ears.

"It's like 7:30. Your man sent me back here to wake you up to cook, bitch. I thought your ass was dead."

"Girl, I totally forgot about going to the beauty supply with you, I'm sorry." I stood up and stretched a little, trying to wake the fuck up so I could make this bum and myself some food.

"It's cool. So how long are you gonna let that nigga live off of you?"

"He doesn't really live off of me, Paige. The only thing I do for him is pay his cellphone, cook, buy groceries, and a few electronics and wardrobe items for him. He helps with rent and utilities."

"How? He doesn't even have a fucking job!"

"Lower your voice! He gets the money from his mother. But that's the least of our problems, he has no fucking ambition. I like a man with goals, a nigga who gets his bread by any means. Russell is just a bum. But we have history."

"And you say Tatiana has it bad," she scoffed.

"She does and so do I. I've never said my relationship was better than hers, Paige. I don't see you with a man though."

"Look I'm good. I have a great job, doing what I love so I couldn't care less about what these weak ass Cleveland niggas have to offer. All of them are the same anyway. Either they're broke, cheaters, or they whoop your ass. I'm good on all three!"

My sister and I were close, very close. She was my best friend outside of Tatiana, even though she and I thought very differently. For as long as I'd known Paige she had always been hard on the opposite sex. Any little thing a nigga did, she was ready to drop their ass, and she tried to make Tatiana and I be the same way. Tatiana was a hopeless romantic though so she always tries to find the good in these trash ass niggas like Brevin. But me on the other hand, well you already know.

"Hopefully one day Tatiana and I will move on." I smiled.

"I hope so. I mean Brevin is that nigga out here in Ohio, but he ain't worth the headache."

"I do remember someone being interested in him before he got with Tati."

"That was before I knew how he was and once I found out, my crush ended like that!" she snapped her fingers and fixed her jeans.

Paige was beautiful and unlike me, she was thicker than a snicker. She had hips, ass, thighs, and big titties. Her stomach wasn't flat, but it didn't matter because she was still bad. She had a light golden complexion like me, and we looked a lot alike. The only difference was that she had the body of a video vixen and I didn't, at all. We had the same parents, but somehow I didn't get blessed like her. It didn't stop the niggas from trying to holler at me though.

Anyway, when Brevin first started making waves as owning Cleveland in a sense, Paige, like every other bitch out here was on him. She couldn't get close to him though, and when she finally lucked up, he dissed her ass for Tatiana. She liked to pretend that she never wanted him like that, but there was a time when all she talked about was him. If I didn't know her so well, I would definitely think she was jealous of Tatiana.

"We all know why your crush on Brevin is no longer."

"He ain't curve no damn body, aight? He actually tried to get at me on the low, but I turned him down out of respect for Tatiana."

"Yeah right! He barely even noticed you then and he damn sure doesn't now that there are three million females in his face every day."

"Look if you're gonna cook go do it. If Russell looks at me like I'm a meal one more time I'm gonna smack his ass! You need to do better with him."

"Wait, weren't you just telling me to move on?" I frowned.

"Yes, but if you're gonna be with the nigga at least be a good damn girlfriend. He's out there looking like a starved dog!"

"Whatever, Paige."

My sister walked, talked, moved, and looked like a hater, but something was stopping me from believing that she was one. I mean she had nothing to be jealous of… right.

CHAPTER TWO

Teflon

I woke up in the hotel bed feeling well rested. I had some shit to take care of later today, but for now I needed to clean up and get some food. After laying there for a couple of minutes, I grabbed my phone to see a plethora of calls from Kayla, Promise, Merce, a couple un-stored numbers, and a text in WhatsApp from Thomas. I wanted to get myself together before returning anything though.

Climbing out of the bed, I brushed my teeth with the toothbrush and paste the hotel gave you, and then hopped into the shower. I planned to take another one when I got home, but I didn't want to risk Kayla being extra and detecting some shit. Once I was all cleaned up, I threw on what I wore the day before and left out, headed home.

When I got into my car, I dialed Merce back to find out why he'd called me after texting Thomas back in the app. It felt so weird using an app to text, but since Thomas was over in Europe, this was the only way he and I could communicate.

"What did you want?" I asked Merce once he picked up, as I pulled out of the parking lot.

"Nigga, they got Luis."

"Fuck you mean they got Luis?" I frowned, almost running a damn red light because I was beyond perplexed.

"Nigga, Diego just called me and said the warehouse was blown up. Luis was inside waiting for us to come to the meeting."

"Why? We're not supposed to meet for another fucking hour. Shit! So what now?"

"I don't know man. Diego wants to talk though and see how we can work through this shit you know."

"Diego? Don't nobody wanna fuck with Diego. He don't know shit, which is why Luis was in charge. I don't have time for this bullshit man."

"I know, Tef, but chill. Let's just hear the man out and see what he has to say before we write him off aight? We meet him in two hours."

"Aight," I sighed before hanging up, just as I was pulling into my condo in Torrance.

I grabbed my phone and keys, then exited the car so I could go inside and get ready for this meeting. I saw Kayla's car parked in the driveway, so she clearly wasn't going into work today. When I opened the front door I saw three brown boxes sitting in the middle of the living room. Peeking into one, I realized it was full of my clothes, shoes, boxers, and socks.

"Kayla!" I hollered to the back and she came walking into the living room with her eyebrow raised. I hated when she did that shit because I knew that meant she was ready to go at it.

"Yes?" she folded her arms.

"Why are you packing my shit up?"

"Because it's time for you to go Tre'Wayne," she replied, using my government. Here we fucking go with this shit.

"Time for me to go? I pay the fucking bills so if anybody should be getting out it's yo' ass!" I grabbed what I needed from some of the boxes so I could go shower. I was already upset about this Luis shit and this right here was not making it any better.

"Oh I am leaving, but you're leaving first until I find a new place. I expect you to continue to pay the bills until I go."

I burst into laughter before she even finished talking and slammed the bathroom door in her face so I could get a good ass scrub down. Once I was clean to my liking, I re-brushed my teeth, flossed, and then rinsed with some mouthwash. I walked out of the bathroom, taking what I'd collected from the boxes, and entered the bedroom we shared to see Kayla sobbing.

"Kayla, what's the damn problem?"

"What's the problem?" she looked up at me with tears in her eyes and confusion written all over her face. Her light complexion was flushed. Pushing her dark hair to the back she said, "You stayed out all night! You think I don't know what the fuck you were doing?" her eyelids lowered.

"I was working—"

"You were not working, Tre'Wayne German! My friend already told me she saw you at the strip club on Western! She also said she saw you leave with two of the fucking strippers!"

"What you want me to do shorty? I told you that I love you and I do, but I just can't be what you want me to be. I will move out, okay?" I was gonna continue to lie but I was exhausted and caught anyway.

"Why can't you, Teflon?" she whimpered.

"I don't have the discipline I guess." I slipped my boxers up and then grabbed my jeans. "I have tried, you know I have but I haven't been able to fight the temptation."

"It's because you need to stop hanging with Merce."

"It ain't his fault what I do, Kayla, and you know that. I'm a grown ass man; I can't be blaming another nigga for how I act." I sighed, trying to calm myself down before saying, "Baby I'm sorry and I love you. I love you enough to allow you to move on if you feel like this ain't what you want."

"I want you, but not this way," she sniffled.

"I know." I took her hands into mine. "Maybe I need some time. We may need some time apart and then come back to one another." I pulled her into me after slipping my jeans on.

"I don't want to be apart from you Tef, but I can't do this anymore. I need you to be faithful to me and if you can't I have to go. It's been too long and too many chances given."

"I hear you," I said in a low tone.

I loved Kayla, I really did. There was no reason not to love her. Not to mention the fact that she actually loved a nigga. I didn't want her to leave, but she was right, I'd been given too many chances. She and I had been together for years and we'd been bickering over my fidelity issues since day one. Believe me I wanted to be better and every time that she forgave me I felt like I could. Then a week later, I would run into a pretty ass bitch that I just couldn't pass up. I *could* control myself I guess, but the problem seemed to be that I didn't want to.

"Promise me you will focus on getting yourself together and not being in another relationship." She smiled.

"I promise. Do you honestly think I would make someone else my woman, Kayla? Only person that I've ever wanted to be in a relationship with is you."

She blushed and smiled before nodding her head.

"I love you, Teflon."

"I love you too Kayla. And I promise a nigga is gonna get it together. Don't give my pussy away." I bit my lip before kissing her sensually. My dick came to life instantly, prompting my hands to rub up under her shirt.

"No, Tef," she whispered.

"Just one more time, baby, please." I sucked on her neck as I played with her nipples.

"No, Tef, go." She shoved me back lightly, fixing her clothes in the process. I could see that she was on the verge of crying so I just decided to leave her alone.

I pecked her lips once more, and then pulled my shirt over my head.

"I'm gonna sleep in the guest room tonight, but tomorrow I will go to a hotel, aight?" I stared down into her face and she nodded before wiping her nose.

I kissed her forehead gently and then left the condo to meet with Diego. Today was just not my fucking day.

CHAPTER TWO

Calvin "Merce" Capers

"I really don't wanna hear anything this nigga has to say." Teflon shook his head as soon as I got into his car.

"Well you should want to because we need to make money. How the fuck we gon' eat if we don't continue on without Luis?" I frowned.

"It'll be hard to do."

We started working for Luis, a couple years back, which is why Teflon and I moved from Ohio to California. We weren't getting money like we wanted to in Cleveland, so when Luis offered for us to come out here and be his killers, we agreed.

We made about one hundred thousand dollars per job at the most, depending on whom we had to kill or take down and how dangerous it was. Now that Luis was gone, we still needed to make sure that our money flow wouldn't slow up at all. I admit, like Teflon I was worried that Diego would be on some bullshit. Luis told us many times how his brother was incompetent and only allowed to roll with him because he was his blood. I wasn't too fond of the idea of him being in charge, but

I wanted to be optimistic because I loved the cash I was getting.

We made it to the Hilton Hotel where Diego asked us to meet him. We secured our heat in our waists and then got out of the car. We spotted him sitting in the plush ass lobby holding a drink and he smiled when he saw us. That was an odd reaction to have since his brother had just been killed earlier today. Something was off about this nigga. I erased the thoughts from my mind because I only wanted to focus on getting paid and nothing else.

"What happened?" Teflon frowned as he and I both took a seat after greeting Diego and some of Luis' men.

"I am not sure. Some of Luis' security said they were sitting outside watching the warehouse, when all of a sudden it caught on fire."

"Is there a body?" I asked because I was suspicious.

Diego stared at me before chuckling lightly. He then pulled his phone out, tapped the screen a few times, and then showed me a picture of Luis' burnt ass body. Somehow, his ring had survived the whole fire, but it was obvious that it was him because of it. He offered to show Teflon, but he waved it off, not interested.

"So what's the deal now?" Teflon questioned.

"Things will continue as planned boys. When someone needs to be taken out I will let you know and you will be paid your regular fee."

"Shouldn't we start finding out who set the fire then? I didn't know of any enemies that Luis had, that were aware of his warehouse."

"No, I will call you when I need you to do anything, okay?" Diego polished off his drink and stood up, fixing his tuxedo coat.

Teflon and I just nodded in response and watched him leave. We went ahead and ordered a drink from the waitress and then sat in silence for a few.

"So what are you thinking?" I quizzed.

"I don't even know. Something ain't right with this shit. He's smiling and upbeat as if his brother didn't just die this morning. I ain't got time for the snake shit."

"Me either my nigga. But right now we don't really have any choices other than him so we need to make the best of the bullshit until we do."

"Agreed," he nodded as the waitress set down our drinks. "So it's a wrap between Kayla and me."

"For how long? A day or two?" I scoffed and sipped my drink. Them niggas were always breaking up and the longest they'd stayed apart was about three days. I didn't take the shit seriously any more; I don't even think they did.

"Nah it's for real this time. I walked in and she had my shit packed up in boxes."

"So, fuck does that mean?"

"I'm fucking serious man. And I think it's for the best. Usually I would try to sweet talk her and shit but this time I just decided to let go. I feel like I'm wasting her time."

"If you love her why can't you just act right?"

"Nigga, I'm wondering the same thing."

"That's why I stay single. I already know what type of nigga I am, and I know I ain't ready. But unlike you, if I do find the one I'm gonna straighten the fuck out."

"I'll get her back." He half smiled as he stared off slurping his drink.

My phone buzzed in my pocket and I looked down to see it was my little brother's homeboy, William. *What the fuck is he calling me for?* I wondered as I hit the green button to answer.

"Merce man, come to the crib! Yo' brother is getting arrested!" he hollered into the phone, making me stand up instantaneously.

"On my way." I quickly hung up and stormed out to the car with Teflon on my heels.

"What happened? Who was that?" he cranked the car up and backed out in a hurry. He didn't know what was going on, but he knew to put a move on it.

"Go to William's crib on Slauson and 54th!"

He did as I asked and peeled out of the Hilton Hotel parking lot. After dipping through the streets, speeding through yellow lights, and cutting niggas off, we were finally hooking a right onto 54th street, which was swarmed with police cars.

"What the fuck is going on?" Teflon yelled as he swooped into an empty park across the street from William's home.

"Sebastian man," I sighed, climbing out. I heard Teflon suck his teeth as he did the same.

My little brother Sebastian had always been a fucking troublemaker. It seemed like from the time his ass was born he was getting into shit. Back in Ohio, where we grew up, he was always fighting and shit, or getting expelled from school. Now Teflon and I obviously weren't any stand up kids, but Sebastian took it to a whole new level, and to make matters worse he was stupid about the shit.

When he begged to come to California with me, my mom and dad protested, but I convinced them to let him go so that he could start fresh. But when they got word about this, they were gonna fly down here and kill my ass. They already blamed me for every damn thing he did or got caught up in.

"Stand back!" an officer shouted as he walked my laughing brother to the police vehicle. This nigga found it funny that he was being arrested.

"Call Luis or some shit!" he had the nerve to yell out to me before being placed in the back seat of the car.

"Shit! Call me as soon as you get a chance!" I stormed onto the sidewalk as the police car sped off the street with others following him.

"What happened, Will?" Teflon frowned.

"He got caught trying to sell coke to an undercover police officer man. I told his ass old boy was suspicious."

"How did he even get ahold to that product?" I questioned William further.

"Beats me. But can't y'all get him out quickly or some shit? Don't Luis have pull with law enforcement?"

"Luis is dead, Will. And mind ya fucking business, aight?" I grimaced and then headed back towards Teflon's car.

"Call Diego and see what he can do," Teflon suggested once we were back in the vehicle.

"I will." I nodded.

Was this shit really happening right now?

***

Some hours later...

I sat on my couch in my condo with Teflon as we smoked our own blunts. We had three more rolled up, and we planned to get high as hell with them. Today had been stressful as fuck for us both and it seemed like California had been a bust. Yeah it was good for a bit, but now it seemed that everything was blowing up in our faces.

I tapped Diego's number and then placed it between my shoulder and cheek as I took a pull on the blunt. By the fifth ring, he picked up and I heard bitches in the background and him chuckling. This nigga surely wasn't acting like his brother had just been burned to death.

"Merce, what can I do for you?"

"Aye man, I was wondering if you could handle something for me. My brother got arrested today and I need you to—"

"Umm, I have a lot going on right now my friend. I can't really think about your brother when my brother is dead. I will see what I can do but it won't be immediate assistance. Okay?"

"It only takes a phone call."

"I have to go."

"Fuck you Diego." I hung up and when I looked over at Teflon, his eyes were bucked, making me laugh. He eventually joined me before taking a huge pull on his blunt. "I can't rock with his fraud ass dog."

"Well if you ain't then neither am I."

"So now what then?"

"We'll think of something," he blew the smoke out and then began ordering pizza from the app on his phone.

Working for Diego Abarca was not gonna happen.

I Got Your Back ◆ *Teflon & Tatiana's Love Story*

CHAPTER TWO

Tatiana

One week later…

It was around 8pm and I was just getting home from doing some planning for this football player's party. My feet were killing me, I was hungry, and I was tired. All I wanted to do was lie down and eat; I didn't even care about what or who Brevin was doing with his stupid ass.

I tried to be sympathetic since his homies died, but I was realizing that he was using that as an excuse to act even funnier than he was acting before. I loved the baby in my body already, but a tiny part of me wishes that I had gotten away and made it with another nigga.

"Welcome home love," Brevin walked up to me, taking my coat and bag. He hung my jacket up and then grabbed my hand to lead me to the kitchen. On the table were two plates of food, candles, and a small gift box.

"Brevin," I whined, on the verge of crying.

This nigga was smart. He knew how to work me if he thought I was getting fed up with him. I guess he could sense the distance I was trying to put between us because he'd gone all out. On the plates, he had my favorites, lobster tails, macaroni and cheese, cornbread, and greens. His mother must have cooked this shit because he couldn't make a pot of top ramen.

"Sit down beautiful." He kissed my lips and pulled the chair out for me.

"What is all of this for, Brevin?"

"For you. I wanted to do this as an apology for the way I've been acting. I'm just stressed about the fact that my homies are gone and the fact that I don't have my killers. But I shouldn't have taken that out on you, Tati."

I smiled widely as we held hands to pray. Once we finished, I immediately started digging in. My eyes were closed as I took a few bites of the macaroni because it was just that good. Brevin's mother could cook like no other.

"Thank you for all of this honey. It lets me know that you still think about me and want to please me."

"Of course, Tatiana. All I care about is you, the baby, and making my money. All of the other shit really doesn't mean anything to me."

"It better not, especially the hoes."

"Nah, I don't even pay them any mind. I mean I look because I have eyes but I don't touch and that's what's most important, right?" He flashed his pretty smile.

"I guess so, yes." I nodded.

We finished eating our food and then had German chocolate cake for dessert. It was so good that I ended up getting two pieces. After I opened my gift to see a beautiful diamond bracelet, we retired upstairs to have a bath together, before going out into the bedroom to lie down. As soon as we were in the bed, Brevin rolled over and got between my legs. His head immediately connected to my opening, and I threw my head back as he entered me slowly while kissing me deeply.

"Breviiinnn," I moaned, caressing his back.

"You love me?" he questioned and I just nodded, knowing I was about to cum. "How much, Tatiana?"

"So much," I whispered.

He continued moving in and out of me as I touched the sides of his sexy face. I loved Brevin, I really did but I wasn't sure if I loved him as much as I used to. He'd done so much and it was hard to forget it all just because of one nice night. In a couple of days or so he would be right back on his bullshit, telling himself that another nice night would have me back on his side again.

"Fuck," he grunted, so I knew he was about to cum.

He sped up, and just as my pelvis tightened, he let loose inside of me. I came right after him and we laid there kissing for a little bit. For some reason, I felt weird as he rolled off me and fell asleep. Usually after we made love, I felt good, refreshed, happy… but I felt disgusted with myself in this moment. He'd done nothing to earn my forgiveness but have his mama cook for me and yet I let him fuck me.

Sometimes I felt like I was just existing in this relationship and not really making anything of it. I mean yes we had a baby coming, but I wasn't even as excited as I felt I should have been. I almost despised the fact that I was having his child. I should have just thanked my lucky stars when I lost the first baby and moved on. That's not to say that I was happy to have had a miscarriage because I definitely wasn't. It's just that I felt like God was giving me a sign and a chance to break free from this union but I didn't take it.

I could pray to him right now for things to get better between Brevin and me, but I wasn't sure if that was what I wanted. If I was being perfectly honest, I wanted to date and see what else was out there, but I couldn't. I was pregnant and a part of me did want to stay with Brevin and be a family. I had these same damn conflicting thoughts every night.

"What you thinking about?" He woke up and rubbed his luminous curly hair.

"Nothing," I whispered.

He smirked at me and then went under the covers, putting his head between my legs. My body immediately responded to his soft lips and tongue toying with my clit. Biting down on my lip, I let out a soft moan as he continued to feast on my center. I hated that he could control me with his sex game, I really did.

"Mmm, aaah!" I gasped and quivered once I released. Planting kisses on my lower lips, he licked between my folds a few times before coming up for air.

After brushing his teeth, he got back into the bed, kissed my cheek, and then dozed right back off. I was about to do the same, but I heard his phone chime. I was gonna ignore it, but my mind wouldn't let me. I got out of the bed slowly, because I didn't want to move too much and wake him. Creeping around the bed to his side, I picked his phone up to see it was a text from someone named Amanda. I didn't know his password, nor was I aware of what finger he used for the scanner, so I just grabbed his iPad. There was a lock on the iPad, but he had the preview feature on, unlike with his phone.

Amanda: Hey baby, what happened to you coming by this morning?

Shaking my head as I read the text over and over, I laid the device in my place and went to sleep in the guest room. Brevin and I were a done deal; I just needed to figure out my next move.

CHAPTER THREE

Teflon

"Groove what's good? What you doing out here?" I let my paternal cousin from Ohio in. He was looking a bit distressed, so I knew it must've been important for him to come all the way out here.

"Now that Luis is gone, who are you working for?" he questioned as he sat down and dapped Merce up.

"We were gon' rock with his bitch ass brother but fuck all of that shit," Merce scoffed as he lit the blunt. "Why?" He blew out smoke.

"Because my boy needs some killers back in Ohio, and I told him I knew some people who could handle the job."

"What's his name? And what does he do?" I quizzed, taking a seat. Kayla caught my eye as she sauntered through the living room and out the door, not bothering to say goodbye.

"Brevin. He's a drug dealer but not the low level kind. Brevin holds the reigns in Cleveland, therefore he needs people to protect him and of course handle enemies."

"Who was he using before?" Merce frowned.

"Remember Mook and Tone? Them, but they recently were killed over some bullshit. We had a minor territory war and Brevin fucked some guy's bitch."

"You call that bullshit? I would've shot at his ass too if he touched mine. But what's the money looking like?" I took a gulp of my water, waiting for Groove to answer.

"Depends on the severity of the job y'all know that, but I told him you two were the real deal and it wouldn't be cheap. He doesn't care, he just… he just wants y'all."

"You mean he's just scared. So we're fucking with a bitch ass nigga in a sense," I chuckled along with Merce.

"He ain't a bitch, he just has his priorities fucked up at times. All he cares about is fucking hoes. And he'll not take care of his shit if a bitch calls," Groove explained.

Now I was a nigga who loved women, but I never put that shit over business. That was some hoe ass nigga shit. My bread always came first, unless it had something to do with Kayla. But I would never postpone getting paid for one of these random hoes out here.

"I don't know about working for a nigga like that." Merce shook his head, reading my mind. I wasn't in the business of doing shit for a nigga who couldn't do it himself. Especially when it sounded like he started problems and was reckless.

"Look just meet with him and see if it's a good fit. Brevin has a lot of money and he needs y'all. I'm sure he would be willing to pay whatever. And y'all niggas know you miss Ohio." Groove smirked.

"How you meet this nigga?" I furrowed my brows.

"His mom and my mom are cool so I used to hang with him here and there. He came up though because he was smart about the way he moved. Brevin is an intelligent ass nigga, but with all the money and women in his face, it's hard for him to focus."

"We'll meet with him but no promises," I sighed and Groove smiled widely as hell.

Brevin didn't sound like a nigga I wanted to work for, but outside of that there were plenty of reasons why I wanted to go back to Cleveland. My family was there and it sounded like Brevin would be willing to pay anything to protect his life. There wasn't nothing like a nigga in need. I smiled as I thought about it.

Two weeks later...

Cleveland, Ohio

We were now out in Cleveland, ready to meet with this Brevin Williamson cat. Groove had been keeping in contact with me since the day he flew back out here to make sure I hadn't changed my mind.

Merce and I talked to Diego and let him know that most likely we'd be moving, and I guess you can say he wasn't fucking with that idea at all. He threatened us, but that shit didn't faze me one bit. No nigga pumped fear in my heart and Diego would have to learn that the hard way. Nobody told me what the fuck to do, nor did I look to anyone for permission. Diego could go fuck himself.

As Merce and I were waiting outside of the airport, a black Escalade pulled up and the back door opened. Groove stepped out grinning, so we dapped him up before letting the driver put our luggage in the trunk. We brought enough clothes for a month just in case, and if we decided to stay we would fly back out and get the rest. I didn't really need my furniture and shit, and I told Kayla she could have it if and when she moved.

Speaking of Kayla, she was highly perturbed when she found out I was planning to move. I didn't know why, since we discussed that we were going our separate ways. We spoke as if we planned to get back together, but over these past few weeks, I hadn't been feeling that idea. I was enjoying the fact that I was free and could work as late as I needed to, or party as late as I wanted to without getting blown up or cursed out. It's childish I know, but it's also the truth. Plus, she made sure to let me know that she was gonna be entertaining other niggas, so how could she expect me to stick around for that? I was good and I wished her the best.

"We're headed to his crib in Ohio City." Groove snapped me from my thoughts as he popped open a bottle of Bourbon for us.

"Oh yeah. I'm guessing his crib is nice as hell," I replied.

"Very nice. Have y'all looked for any places to stay?"

"Nah, we're gonna do the hotel thing until we're sure about the move. We need to get through this meeting first before anything," Merce answered.

"I'm telling y'all this shit is a go. Y'all belong in Cleveland, not uppity ass Cali." Groove chuckled and so did we.

"Cali was cool, but like I said, we will see how this goes. From what you told me Brevin sounds soft, so I need to feel him out myself." I stared out the window, admiring my hometown.

After a while, we finally made it to a nice ass crib in Ohio City. I was sure it was at least eight bedrooms in that bitch and I could tell it was built at Brevin's request. It didn't look like the others on the block, it stood out, which I'm sure was the purpose.

The driver pulled into the driveway on the side and then hopped out to let the three of us out. Groove led us to the front door, slipped his key in, and then we followed him in. As we were walking through the kitchen, a girl came in dressed in a sports bra, tights, and tennis shoes. Her hair was up in a ball on her head, and she was sweating a little. Her stomach was poking out, not too much, but I could tell it was a baby in there because of her little frame. I swear my heart stopped for a little bit as she and I made eye contact. I had never seen someone as pretty as her and I'd seen a lot of women in my twenty-eight years.

"Teflon," I just had to introduce myself. The fact that she was pregnant didn't even bother me for some reason. As sexy as she was I would raise that muthafucka as my own.

"Tatiana." She half smiled as her eyes darted from mine to Groove and then Merce. "Are you guys here to see Brevin?" she removed her hand from my grasp. I couldn't take my eyes off of her, no matter how hard I tried, and I could tell my gaze made her uncomfortable.

"Yeah, tell him that we'll be in the den area and that I have Teflon and Merce with me."

"Okay." She nodded and turned to leave, but not before we made awkward eye contact again. How did a nigga like Brevin bag that? I will never fucking know. I shook my head and exhaled as I followed Groove and Merce to the den.

"That's Brevin's girl?" I quizzed as soon as we sat down in the den.

"Yep, Tatiana Drew. She's beautiful, huh?" Groove smirked.

"Nigga, that's a fucking understatement," I looked towards the entrance of the den as if she were right there. Shit I wish she were right there.

I usually liked my girls thick and Tatiana wasn't, but she was just as fine to me. Her skin color was golden but with a hint of cinnamon, something I hadn't seen before. She had a mole on her left cheek and her brown eyes were a beautiful shade of chocolate. Her breasts weren't big and neither was her butt, but she wasn't skinny per say. She was small but perfect. I'd never been so horny in my life.

"Good afternoon fellas, sorry to take so long." Brevin walked in with his pretty ass girl right behind him.

"It's cool," Merce responded but my attention was focused on Tatiana. Her name was even sexy. I'd heard the name plenty of times, but this time it sounded different.

"Would you guys like something to drink? I will be making lunch once I get dressed," she offered. Her voice was sweet and sexy coming from her full lips.

"Yeah baby, bring us some Hennessy please," Brevin kissed her lips before coming to sit down like us. "So Teflon and Merce, my man Groove here told me a lot about you two."

"He told us a lot about you too. We know your last people got blazed," Merce squinted his eyes, wanting an explanation. The one Groove gave wasn't good enough for either of us.

"Yeah I um, made some poor choices. You know niggas get in their feelings when you fuck their bitch and take over their territory."

This nigga had Tatiana and was fucking other bitches? Wow. I mean I wasn't any better for how I dogged Kayla, but it made me cringe knowing that this nigga was doing Tatiana dirty. I definitely wanted to fuck his bitch, but she deserved better than that, just like Kayla. Tatiana was the type you married and stayed on the good foot with. She didn't need to be with a nigga like me nor Brevin.

"Well we don't mind coming on board as long as the money is right, but we would prefer it if…"

I lost my train of thought when Tatiana entered the den with our drinks. She removed my glass from the tray, and when she handed it to me, I made sure to touch her small soft hands with mine. We looked into one another's eyes but she was quick to lose that eye contact. I could already imagine pinning her hands behind her head as I beat her pussy up while she called out my name. I took a gulp of my drink to calm my dick down.

"You would prefer it if what?" Brevin quizzed as Tatiana finished passing the drinks out.

"If you didn't do things that put your life in jeopardy."

"Understandable, so do we have a deal?"

"What will the money be like?" Merce quizzed.

"For small jobs $30,000 and for big jobs it'll be $120,000. That's the cap," he responded.

"You got a deal," I said.

"Great, where are you guys staying? Have you found a place to live yet?"

"Nah, we booked a hotel for the time we'll be here. We'll be looking though for sure," Merce replied.

"Why don't you guys stay here until then? I'm hot right now and I wouldn't be surprised if these niggas found out where I lived. I got seven bedrooms, fully furnished with personal bathrooms in each. I have a chef, maid, a—"

"Sounds good," I cut him off. I didn't care if this was a one-bedroom shack in Buckeye-Shaker, the fact that Tatiana lived here was the only amenity I needed.

"Cool, cool." Brevin chuckled excitedly with his scaredy cat ass.

Like I said before, I had plenty of reasons to come back here and Tatiana had just been added to that list. I wasn't sure what I was gonna do, but I just knew that I had to be close to her. I didn't wanna be her man because she deserved better than me, but I had to have her in my circle one way or another.

CHAPTER THREE

Tatiana

That night…

I'd just finished taking a nice shower, and when I walked into the bedroom, Brevin was coming in. I smiled at him uncomfortably because my thoughts had me oozing with guilt. That man earlier, Teflon, had me feeling things I should only feel for Brevin. I didn't even know his ass, but I wanted to be in his presence. I wanted to know everything there was to know about him.

"Did you have fun?" I asked Brevin as I began to spread lotion all over my legs.

"Fun? I guess. We mainly talked business and stuff. I told them they could stay here, Merce and Teflon, in the guest bedrooms. I didn't introduce you huh?"

"No need, Groove did," I half lied.

He smiled and neared me, before kissing on my neck. I wasn't in the mood, well I was, but not for him. And now hearing that Teflon would be staying here in this home with us had me feeling very hot and very bothered.

"I'm gonna get a snack," I nudged Brevin off me and darted towards the door. I heard him groan but I ignored it. Suddenly he was the least of my worries.

I made my way down the hall, checking the two bedrooms located down there. No one was inside, so I went downstairs to check those. The very last door was cracked open and when I walked by I saw him. He was the sexiest nigga I'd ever seen. He had smooth brown skin, kinky hair, a scruffy beard, and beautiful slanted eyes. He had to be half Asian or something. He was very tall, taller than Brevin so about 6'4, and at the moment his shirt was off so I could see his tattoos, abs, and strong chest. I felt like a voyeur as I watched him unpack things. My eyes traveled down his strong arms, admiring his sleeve and the iced out watch on his wrist. I hated the fact that I was so attracted to him because I couldn't do anything about it.

"You just gonna stand there like a creep?" he snapped me back to reality. I said nothing for a few moments before entering his room, embarrassed.

"I just wanted to make sure everything was to your liking."

"It is thank you." He bit down on his plump bottom lip and let his eyes travel down my frame. I had on a short silk nightgown with the matching robe. The way he looked at me prompted me to close the robe over myself. "Well goodnight, Teflon."

"Wait, come sit down for a second."

"It's 1am."

"I didn't ask for the time shorty. Come sit down please. Don't make me beg and know that I *will* beg you."

Moving my hair to the other side of my head nervously, I made my way over to him and sat down on the bed. His cologne, which I recognized to be Valentino, permeated the air, making my center salivate slightly. I blinked constantly as he took me in, gazing at me as if I were a painting.

"Where did you come from?" I asked, hoping to pull his eyes from wandering all over me.

"I'm from here, originally, born and raised, but I moved to California for work. That shit blew over so I'm back to work for your man."

"Oh."

"Can I?" he asked, referring to the small bulge in my stomach.

"Umm, sure, I guess so." I nodded nervously. I was so skittish that you'd think I'd never been around a man in my life.

He pulled the belt of my robe to open it, and I held my breath because I wasn't sure what was going to happen next. He took his big hand and placed it against my stomach gently before rubbing. Brevin had never done that and I didn't mind until now. Teflon stared at my stomach as he caressed it, making a small smile creep onto my face.

"How long before it gets here?" he questioned with his eyes still locked on my belly.

"About four and some change." I chuckled.

"You look beautiful pregnant, breathtaking even," he looked

deeply into my eyes, making my breathing become shallow.

"Thank you." I pushed my hair behind my ears. "Do you have any children?" my eyes followed him as he stood up and began removing his jeans… he was so fucking tall like Brevin. "Oh let me go—"

"No, stay. I promise I won't flash you, I'm just getting ready to go shower. I like your company baby girl."

"You don't even know me."

"That's now, give it time. And to answer your question, no I don't have any kids."

"Oh, do you want them?" I tried to keep my attention on his eyes, but seeing that V, which I knew led down to his manhood, temporarily snatched my eyes from his.

"Yeah I do, but I don't know if I will get them. I want kids with a woman that I'm willing to marry and I don't know if I will find that."

His statement turned me off, because I knew that meant he was just like Brevin. He was nothing but a player and oddly that had me feeling some type of way. I had a man so why was I worried about Teflon's affairs anyway? Instead of responding, I just rose to my feet, ready to leave.

"Leaving already?" he raised a brow.

"Yes, it's very late. I'm tired and I have to be up early for pregnancy yoga. You have a goodnight Teflon." I half smiled, retying my robe.

"Aye, thank you for talking to me." He grabbed my hand and brought it up to his perfect lips to kiss the back of it. "Try to make visiting me a habit, Tatiana."

My chest rose and fell slowly but roughly as his hand held onto mine. It felt so good and so right even though it was wrong. He was pulling me in and so quickly. I refused to engage with a man who was no different than the guy I was pregnant by though.

"I will do what I can."

"Okay," he replied so lowly that it was almost inaudible.

His already slanted eyes were low, so I knew he was high and it looked so sexy on him. He watched me the whole time until I closed the bedroom door behind me. Once I did, I inhaled sharply with my eyes closed. Teflon staying here was gonna be bad for my health.

I Got Your Back ◆ *Teflon & Tatiana's Love Story*

CHAPTER THREE

Teflon

I opened my eyes and blinked a couple times, before realizing my dick was hard as fuck and that what had just happened was a dream. I hadn't been able to get Tatiana off my fucking mind since the first time I saw her ass. Granted it had only been less than twenty-four hours, but still that was odd for me. Any woman that wasn't Kayla only stayed on my mind when she was on my dick. Once I nutted I never thought about the bitch again. But Tatiana, I hadn't even touched her, well not in the way that I wanted to, yet her little ass was planted firmly in my mind.

After getting over the fact that I didn't actually fuck, I had only dreamt about it, I reached for my phone on the nightstand. As usual, my lock screen was covered with texts, phone calls, and Instagram DMs. I saw Kayla had hit me a few times, so I decided to return her call while I gathered my shit for another shower.

For some reason for as long as I can remember, I've always taken a shower at night and one in the morning. I felt dirty when I only did one of them.

"Hey I'm guessing you made it since you never called to tell me," Kayla answered.

"Sorry about that Kay, I got busy as soon as I touched down. But yes I'm safe and sound here in this mansion."

"Mansion?"

"Yeah the guy I'm working for is allowing Merce and me to stay here until we find our own place."

"I know you're hating that arrangement," she chuckled. *Not as much as you'd think.*

"Yeah, you know me. But look I have some shit to take care of Kay, so I will talk to you some time later aight?"

"When?"

"Kayla, I thought we were over? We can't act like we're in a relationship when we're not. Have a good day baby girl and I will hit you sooner than later."

"Fuck you, Tre'Wayne." She hung up in my face.

She confused the fuck out of me I swear. She was the main one wanting to end shit with me, but now she was mad because I didn't want to text and talk all damn day? I didn't do that shit when we were together, so why would I do it now that weren't? I didn't know her reasoning and honestly I didn't really care. I left Kayla and our relationship problems back in California.

I dug through my bag for some boxers, a white polo, some dark jeans, socks, and then my all white Chucks. I was never a flashy dresser, but I was a clean one if that made sense. Once I had my outfit laid out, I brushed my teeth and then hopped into the shower. I put on my clothes, and as I was putting lotion on my elbows, I heard a knock at the door.

"Come in!" I yelled out.

"I just finished getting dressed too." Merce cheesed widely before coming over to dap me up. "I'm about to go run an errand with Groove though, you wanna come?"

"It depends. Is Tatiana still here?"

"Nigga I don't know. Maybe, she *does* live here. Why does it matter though?" he beamed, already knowing the answer to his question. "You gon' fuck the man's girl in his own damn house, Tef?"

"I ain't say nothing about fucking, I just wanna be her friend. You know be a shoulder to lean on and if she happens to want some dick too… I will turn her down."

"Turn her down? Nigga, what pipe is you smoking. She bet not come to me begging for some dick because I'm gon' fuck the shit out of her," he sucked his teeth before we both laughed.

"Oh excuse me; if you guys are hungry there is breakfast over in the kitchen."

The Greek goddess herself walked into my bedroom looking even sexier than she did yesterday, which at the time I thought was impossible. She had on a light pink dress that clung to her small frame, accentuating her pregnant belly, which was still rather small. Her dark brown curly hair was down, sweeping the top of her shoulders. I loved super long hair, but the fact that hers wasn't didn't bother me. She was nothing like the women I usually gravitated towards, so I was a bit confused on why I was so captivated by her. I mean yeah her face was beyond beautiful, but I preferred my women to be stacked. She wasn't though, yet she was perfect to me.

"Thank you," Merce and I replied in unison as we both smiled at her. She gave us a half smile and left out of the room.

"That nigga Brevin is a fool to let niggas be around her," Merce said exactly what I was thinking. "Anyway, I will be back, hopefully that nigga Brevin will be awake by then."

"Or not." I chuckled as we both left out of the room.

We made our way downstairs to see Tatiana sitting at the table with another pretty ass girl. Got damn, where the fuck were they when I lived here? I mean Cleveland had some bad ones, but these two right here were on some other shit. Shorty at the table had a golden brown complexion, dark auburn hair, appeared to have a small frame like Tatiana, and big pretty eyes. I looked over to Merce and I could tell he was thinking exactly what I was.

"Merce," he introduced himself to her and I wanted to go and pick her jaw up for her. *I don't know why she was gaping at this ugly ass nigga.* I laughed to myself at my thoughts.

"Jadynn," she finally replied.

"Nice to meet you," Merce bit down on his lip as he continued to look down into her eyes. "Oh this is my boy Teflon."

I shook her hand and then started making myself a plate as Merce left out. Jadynn watched him the whole way and then turned to look at Tatiana. I wasn't sure what the look meant exactly, but I was sure it had something to do with her being attracted to my boy.

"So what do you ladies have planned for today?" I sat next to Tatiana purposely.

"Well we have to work on an event we're throwing at Mellow Nightclub. It's for the new Cincinnati Bengals player Jason Coral," Tatiana explained.

"Yeah, you and your friend should come. We can get you a ticket," Jadynn offered.

"I don't really know if that's my scene," I stuffed some bacon into my mouth as my eyes ran amuck all over Tatiana.

"Same thing Brevin says. He never comes so I didn't expect you to want to come either. You guys are in the same boat." Tatiana grinned.

"You know what get us the tickets, Jadynn."

Upon hearing that Brevin wouldn't be there, I suddenly wanted to go. I would be alone with Tatiana and that's exactly what I needed. I didn't give a fuck if Brevin knew I was checking for his girl, but I knew *she* cared.

I could tell right off the bat that she was one of those girls who stayed faithful to men who didn't deserve it, like Kayla. The only difference here was that she made me want to do better. It was sad to say, considering the fact that Kayla never made me want to try. I'd thought about it, but Tatiana had me actually willing to put forth some effort. She gave me some newfound faith in myself. Anyway, having her away from Brevin may make her open up to me some more.

"Great, one for you and one for Merce," Jadynn flashed her pretty smile and nodded giddily. I turned my attention to Tatiana and we both gave each other a smirk.

That same evening...

"Man, take his drunk ass upstairs," Merce scoffed to Groove.

Merce, Groove, Brevin and I all went to one of Brevin's groupie's house to chill. None of us wanted to go, but because Merce and I were getting paid to make sure nobody killed his weak ass, we had to accompany him. It was cool because we did get to play cards and shit, and it got even better when Brevin and old girl went to the room and let us be.

It did bother me to know he was cheating on my future wife, but I wasn't one to talk. Kayla would slap the shit out of me if I tried to point the finger at Brevin. Anyhow, this nigga got twisted as fuck and almost threw up on me until I put a gun to his head and told him he'd better swallow it.

"He's a fucking mess." Merce shook his head as we headed to our rooms.

"I'm already tired of his ass. In a minute I'm gon' let whoever is looking for him kill his ass." We chuckled in unison.

"That doesn't sound too bad. Well I'm about to change and go meet up with this chick I met earlier and get some pussy to relieve my stress."

"You do that. I got a couple hitting me up, old ones that I used to bang out when I lived here. They said they saw you out and about earlier so they knew I was here too."

"You're welcome," he winked and then went into his room.

I did the same and began removing my tennis shoes when I heard the front door open. I put them to the side and then tread down the hallway to see who it was, even though I already knew. A smile spread across my face when I spotted Tatiana. Her legs looked so sexy in the heels she had on. I watched her as she sifted through the mail and finally looked up to see me and smirked.

"Are you just gonna stand there and watch me like a creep?" she questioned, using my same words from last night.

"For a little bit. Come talk to me." I nodded back towards my room. "He's drunk as fuck and out of it, come on," I added when I saw her hesitate.

She followed behind me and we ran into Merce who was smiling widely at us.

"Don't worry ma, I didn't see nothing," he said before walking past us.

"He's cool," I reassured her before we continued to my bedroom. When we got in, I closed the door and helped her remove her jacket.

"Maybe you should open the door."

"It's fine. He's asleep and I'm not gonna hurt you. You trust me?"

"What? I don't even know you, how could you ask me something like that?" she frowned, folding her arms.

"I can tell that you know how to read people, Tatiana. Do you think that I would do something to you?" She shook her head 'no' but slowly. "Then you trust me right?" She nodded subtly.

Pulling her to the chaise in the room, I sat her down and began removing her shoes. She inhaled and exhaled quickly and sharply, so I knew she wanted to say something but she changed her mind. Throwing her shoes to the side, I sat on the carpet and began massaging her small feet.

"That feels good," she cooed.

"I'm sure it does." I eyed her sexy legs. "You've been on your feet all day, while being pregnant, that's a lot shorty."

"I know."

"So now it's my turn to pry a little. Where did you come from?" I asked her the same shit she asked me, and in that same odd way.

"I was born in Florida, but my mother gave me up for adoption and my adoptive parents moved to Cleveland when I was two years old."

"They still around?"

"My father is but not my mother. My mother… she…" she cleared her throat.

"You don't have to tell me just yet. I'm a patient man I don't mind waiting," I continued massaging her feet gently. I was fighting the urge to kiss up her legs until I was face to face with her pussy.

"Thanks."

"I can't get over how beautiful you are." She said nothing in response, her eyes just darted away as she nervously pushed her hair behind her ears. I took a chance and let my hand move up her smooth calf, while keeping my eyes on her pretty face. "It's okay if I touch you right?"

"Teflon," she whispered. "I'm tired so I'm gonna go to bed." She pulled her foot from me and stood up, grabbing her shoes along the way.

"I'm sorry; I didn't mean to make you feel uncomfortable."

"It's fine. Look, I don't want you to get the wrong idea, Teflon. I have a man and I'm carrying his child."

"You're stating facts."

"Yes… huh?"

"Why are you telling me that when that's something I already know?"

"Because I-I want to make sure you haven't forgotten that I belong to your boss and that's how things are gonna stay."

"You like me, Tatiana?" I moved closer to her, causing her to gasp lightly.

"I have a boyfriend-- fiancé, a-and a baby."

"That's not what I asked you. Again, you're stating facts. I'm asking you how you feel, do you like me?"

"I just met you."

"Dodging the question," I grinned and moved her hair from her face. She moved from my touch and looked away. "I will leave you alone, goodnight." I opened the door for her and she quickly walked out.

At least for now I would.

CHAPTER THREE

Jadynn

I'd been calling my sister all day because we were supposed to go to dinner tonight when I got off work. She hadn't answered once, which was kind of annoying considering the fact that she'd bugged me for weeks saying I never spent time with her. A part of me didn't even wanna go because I was tired from planning that Jason Coral party all day, but I didn't want my sister thinking that my job came before family. I was tired of her, my mother, and Russell saying that all I did was work.

Swooping into her driveway, I shut the engine off and climbed out. Her car was there so I knew her ass was too. This bitch never let people drive her anywhere because she swore that the only person who knew how to drive was her ass. I didn't mind letting her though because I despised her complaining the whole damn ride when I drove.

"Paiiiggee!" I called out as I banged on her screen door.

I got no response so I was starting to worry. I pulled my keys from my pocket and quickly slipped it into the knob, gaining entrance. I rushed to the back and burst into her room, but man I wish I hadn't.

She was down on her knees sucking my nigga's dick, as he held his head back in pleasure. The way he palmed the back of her head made me want to break each of his fingers, one by one.

"Jadynn! It's not even—" Russell tried to say.

WHAM!

I punched Paige's ass and she flew into her closet, sliding down the door while groaning. I then turned my attention to Russell, who had his hands up and his eyes bucked. I couldn't even cry because I was so damn angry at what the fuck was going on. All I saw was red and only violent thoughts raced through my mind.

"Baby calm down!" he hollered when I chucked Paige's iPad at him.

Immediately after I began taking off on him, while Paige sobbed like a newborn baby on the floor. She was crying as if she'd just caught me with her man. I couldn't believe her. She was my sister and someone I considered a best friend, yet she had betrayed me in the worst way.

All those times she tried to convince me to move on from broke down ass Russell; it was probably because she wanted him to her damn self. These thoughts continued to circle my mind as I wailed on Russell's whack ass. I didn't even care about the blood that I saw coming from his face.

Finally, he got a good grip on my wrists, stopping me from fucking him up.

"Let me go muthafucka!" I shouted and tried to snatch away from him. He wouldn't let me at first so I kicked his ass in his bare nuts.

"Jadynn, I'm so sorry," Paige wept, still sitting on the floor naked.

I walked up to her, backhanded her ass to the point where the other side of her face hit the closet and then left out.

There wasn't shit else for me to say to her or that nigga Russell. I hoped she planned to let him live there because he wasn't coming back to my shit. And whatever he wore over, was all he was gonna have because the shit he had at my spot, he would no longer have access to.

When I got into my car the waterworks started, but I quickly wiped the tears and began backing out. I wasn't so much sad about Russell as I was about Paige doing this to me. She was supposed to have my back, but instead she was creeping with the same nigga she was begging me to leave alone. Something told me she was a hater but I just didn't want to listen and now look at me. And I feel so stupid for sticking by Russell when I knew I should have been let his ass go. But I guess since I didn't want to do it, God did it for me.

I didn't feel like going home so I decided to stop by a bar near my apartment. I knew it wasn't a good idea for me to have a drink and then try to drive home, but I would cross that bridge when I came to it. My mom or Tatiana would come and get me if push came to shove.

When I walked into the bar, I saw the back of someone that looked familiar. Naturally, I wasn't in the mood for company after enduring something so heartbreaking, but strangely I wouldn't mind getting to know him right now. I fixed my purse strap nervously and then made my way over to the bar where he was sitting. I left a stool in between us because I didn't want to be too forward. I then took a deep breath as I set my purse in front of me.

"What will you have?" the bartender questioned me.

"Can I try the jalapeño margarita please?" I sighed and that's when he looked over at me.

I got even more nervous than I already was and I didn't know why. He was sexy as hell, even though he wasn't really my type. He was light skinned, had a scruffy beard, was skinny and very tall like his friend that had a thing for Tatiana. Even though it was late in the evening, he had shades on and a baseball cap with his kinky curly hair sticking out of the back a little.

"Jadynn, right?" he pointed to me with one of his long fingers, allowing me time to admire his diamond watch under the light.

"Yes, you said your name was Merce?" I finally got the courage to look over into his eyes… well shades.

"Yeah that's right. What are you doing here? And without your friend?"

"She can't exactly drink and I wanted to be alone for the time being." I accepted my margarita and mouthed thank you to the bartender.

I tried handing him my card, but Merce said, "Nah, put it on my tab."

"I don't need you to pay for my drink."

"I know. You don't look like a woman who needs much of anything from anybody." I didn't respond so he asked, "Why did you want to be alone?"

"I found something out that really hurt me and I just wanted some alone time to think."

"Well I won't bother you then, it seems like it really got to you." He tossed back the rest of his liquor and then waved to the bartender for a refill.

"No you're not bothering me," I let him know quickly because I wanted him to continue to talk. "Why are you here without your friend Teflon?"

"I just stopped by here on the way home, nothing major like what you got going on over there though. Are you originally from Cleveland?"

"Yes, you?"

"I am, love my city. I should have never left, but I thought I'd found an opportunity down in California. The statement grass ain't greener is so true."

"What kind of an opportunity? A job?"

"Exactly. And truthfully it was going good for a while and then out of nowhere shit went left, so Teflon and I came back."

"I was gonna say I'd seen you before, but I thought you were new to Ohio."

"I'm not. I've never seen you though." He took off his shades and furrowed his bushy eyebrows. He was so rugged and opposite from the clean cut niggas that I usually went for, but I liked it. I liked how raw he was and I knew he was the type of nigga to put it all on the table… that intrigued me.

"How do you know you've never seen me?"

"Trust me shorty I wouldn't have forgotten that face." He chuckled to himself.

"I could've been an ugly duckling and then grew into my looks."

"Well for one I've only been gone for three and a half years and secondly that would be one hell of a transformation from ugly to what you look like now."

"Don't pump my head up, it won't help you."

"Won't help me do what?" He looked thoroughly confused and now I felt dumb for insinuating that he wanted me like… like I wanted him.

"Nothing, it was a joke."

"Well have a goodnight and don't drink too many of those. These niggas around here can get rowdy and I wouldn't want some shit happening to you." Why did that turn me on?

"You're leaving?" I exclaimed, when I really didn't mean to be so excited when I asked.

"Yeah, I have some shit to do in the morning, but it was nice chatting with you. And whatever that nigga did, you deserve better anyway." He winked before pulling his jacket on, grabbing his receipt, and leaving.

Embarrassingly I developed a crook in my neck from trying to watch him through the window as he walked down the sidewalk.

Temporarily, Paige and Russell had left my mind.

CHAPTER FOUR

Merce

As I was leaving the bar, my cellphone rang and I pulled it out to see it was this girl named Savannah. I wasn't even sure how she'd gotten my new number, but I knew hers by heart so it was obvious who was calling me when looked at my phone.

She and I used to fuck around heavy before I left to California and I admit I did think about locking her down a couple times. However, unlike Teflon, I wasn't getting into some shit that I knew I wasn't ready for. When I told Savannah that and brought up the fact that I was moving to California, she told me never to call her ass again. And when I did just that, she got even madder saying I didn't care. I just cut her off completely after that and stopped replying or answering anytime she reached out. She eventually gave up, but she must've gotten word that I was back in town.

"What's good?" I answered before slipping into the rental I'd gotten. I couldn't wait to get my own shit.

"You wasn't gon' tell me you were back in town, Merce?"

"I didn't know we were cool like that anymore for me to be telling you I was town and shit, Sav."

"Well we are. I was just in my feelings before."

"Don't talk like this shit just happened a couple of days ago. We haven't talked in two damn years woman."

"I know and I miss you, us."

"Us, there won't be any of that, I'm gonna tell you right now." I didn't want her getting the wrong impression at fucking all.

"So you're still on that bullshit, Merce? You're twenty-eight years old still trying to run around like some high school kid."

"I'm not trying to do shit but get money and help my family, Savannah. I'm really not trying to be stressed out when I've only been here a couple of fucking days."

She continued talking and running her mouth, but seeing Jadynn walk to her car caught my attention. I cranked my vehicle and then rolled the window down so I could speak to her.

"Have a goodnight!"

She looked to me with a confused expression, but soon after a smile appeared on her pretty face. She pushed her hair behind her ear and reached into her purse for her keys.

"You too," she finally replied.

"Hello! Hellooooo!" Savannah shouted through my phone.

"Look I have to go, I can't drive and talk. I will see you around or some shit."

"Or you could come see me now," she said sweetly. "I just cooked and everything."

"You still live downtown?"

"Close, I live in Central now. Want me to text you the address?"

"Yeah, go ahead and do that."

We disconnected and I sped out of the parking lot of the bar, headed to her crib in Central. I nodded my head in approval once I arrived to her nice little place on Sumpter Court. She was doing pretty well for herself, but I expected nothing less from Savannah. She was always a dope boy's dream because she was that good girl college student that niggas in the hood knew would go places. Savannah never let me forget how lucky I was to have her. I shook my head at my thoughts.

I got out and jogged up her steps before knocking on the little screen door. She answered in no time wearing some little ass shorts, a bra, and was holding a bottle of some type of alcohol that I couldn't make out through the screen.

"Took you long enough," she sucked her teeth.

"I had to stop and get gas," I stated, nonchalantly as I took her place in. It was small but still very nice. I guess she didn't need much room since it was only her anyway.

I followed her to the living room and once I sat down, she went to get some glasses. She filled them with the whiskey and then left out, returning with two plates piled with slices of enchilada pie. She knew that was my favorite, which made me wonder if she had planned to invite me over.

"Thank you, this shit looks fire," I took the plate from her. She just chuckled like she always did when she got a compliment and then we dug in.

"You back for good now?"

"I would like to think so."

"You know if you need work Merce, I can check with my boss to see if he can help you out. Maybe you can be my assistant or something."

"Umm, nah. Can I get some water please? I've had enough alcohol tonight."

She stared at me for a few and then put her plate down on the coffee table to get up. She came back with the water, handed it off, and then took her seat next to me again.

"Why don't you want me to see about getting you a job? Is it your pride?"

"No, it's not." I gulped the water. "I have a job and I don't need you trying to help me out aight?"

"I'm sure whatever that job is, it's something illegal. Merce, I don't want anything to happen to you baby, and running with Teflon and Groove will get you nowhere but behind bars or in a grave." She spoke to the side of my face as I continued to grub on my food and stare straight ahead at the turned off television. "So you're gonna ignore me?"

"I just wanna finish this."

We ate in silence, and once I was done, I polished the water off and stood up. I was ready to go, and confused on why my ass thought coming here was a good idea.

"Calvin stay, I'm sorry." She got up with me and began loosening my belt buckle.

I stared down into her pretty face and then palmed the top of her head to push her down to her knees. She continued unfastening my jeans and once they were open, she reached for my dick. He went right into her warm mouth and I threw my head back in ecstasy. Savannah may have been a good girl, but her head game had always been one of a porn star.

"Shit!" I groaned as I pulled my jacket off.

She kept moving her mouth up and down my shaft. She only stopped so I could pull her bra off. My dick got harder, and I knew I was about to burst, so I gripped her hair and moved her up and down a little faster until I did. She took it down like a champ, and then stood to her feet so I could push her shorts down. She wasn't wearing any panties, and seeing her pussy right there had me damn near biting a hole in my lip.

"Get on all fours, on the couch," I demanded calmly.

She did as I asked and I walked up behind her and ran my fingers across her middle for a little bit. She was wet as fuck and I couldn't wait to get inside. Stepping out of my jeans, I made sure to get the condom from my wallet and roll it down. I gripped her waist and then slid inside of her tight hole slowly.

"Mmm, oh," she whimpered, her voice cracking a little. "I missed you so much, Merce."

I stroked her slowly, enjoying how good she felt. I ran my finger across the tattoo of my name on her lower back, while pounding her spot forcefully but slowly. I let my hands caress her filled out frame, groping her titties and everything as I moved carefully in and out of her walls. Savannah liked it slow at first and that always made her cum the hardest.

"Aaaah," she released that quickly on my pole, causing her body to tense up and quiver.

I clutched her shoulder with one hand and then grabbed her waist with the other before going in. I was slamming into her, watching her ass move all about which was almost too much for me. I kept my stamina in control however. She came once again, getting even wetter, so after delivering some more hardcore pumps, I was filling the condom up.

We both panted for a little bit and then I went to the bathroom to clean myself. She followed, and after I flushed the condom, we decided just to get into the shower together. Afterwards, I had seconds of the enchilada, dessert and then went to sleep in her big ass bed.

Tonight was pretty legit, but strangely I couldn't get Jadynn's beautiful face out of my mind.

CHAPTER FOUR

Tatiana

The next morning…

"Oh, Suzanne you don't have to take that." I smiled at Brevin's and my housekeeper. She was about to go take Teflon his breakfast.

"But Mr. Teflon is awake and I want to have his breakfast in there before he comes out of the shower," she replied.

"You can go on about your day. I will take care of it."

"Okay, thanks Ms. Drew."

I simply nodded before taking the tray into my hands. I was playing with fire trying to do whatever it was that I was doing. I found myself looking for reasons to be near Teflon, even when I knew I shouldn't be. I was pregnant by one man and vying for another. At this moment, I could barely contain my smile as I walked down the hall to his bedroom with the tray of food. Good thing Merce didn't come home last night, because I would hate for him to see me around Teflon's room again.

As usual, Teflon's door was cracked and he was standing there with a white towel wrapped around his waist. The water droplets, which covered his brown skin, made him look so sexy. His tattoos that covered his strong chest, back, and arms were so attractive to me, even though I swore I hated guys who had a lot of them. He was so much more of a thug than Brevin and it was obvious.

"Good morning, I hope you're hungry." I brought the tray in and stood there.

"I am, close the door please."

"Sure." I set the tray of food on his bed and then walked to the door. I was about to leave but he stopped me.

"No you stay, but close the door so I can get dressed."

"In front of me?" I asked as if I were appalled, but closed the door anyway.

"Yeah baby girl, relax. It's only a dick and two balls, I promise," he stated seriously then cheesed. I couldn't help but to smile back.

Instead of watching him get naked in front of me, I walked to the dresser and looked over some of his jewelry. He had a lot of nice watches, some bracelets, earrings, cufflinks, and a couple of chains. I took the top off the Valentino cologne to inhale it, just as he grabbed it from me to spray his bare chest. He had quickly slipped into some boxers, jeans, and socks, before spraying the cologne. I watched him pull a polo over his head, then he sat down to begin eating.

"Have a seat." He said, biting the bacon. I listened. "You missed me?"

"Missed you? I see you damn near everyday. You're living in my boyfriend's home."

"You know what I mean. For the past two nights you haven't visited me in my room and now you bring me breakfast."

"It's just breakfast, it's not like I cooked it."

"Yeah but usually Suzanne brings it."

"What are you implying, Teflon?"

"Nothing, beautiful."

"Don't call me that, I told you to stop talking to me like that." He made me feel things when he called me beautiful or baby girl. It was small I know, but still.

"I'm not talking like anything, I'm simply stating facts. You're a very beautiful woman so I called you that. Chill out, your man trusts you."

"As he should."

"Yep." He nodded as he stuffed his face with forkfuls of waffles. "I'm looking for a new place to move to and I was wondering if you'd come with me today."

"I'm not a real estate agent."

"I know that smart ass. Merce's friend is and she told us this one building has some vacancies. I wanna go see it and I'm asking for you to come."

"Why me?"

"Because I like you and I want to spend time with you."

"Teflon—"

"You asked me why and I told you. Now will you come or not? I'm not asking you to marry me or be with me, I just want some company when I go look."

"Fine, but no flirting."

"I can't promise you that baby. Flirting is natural for me, especially when I'm in the company of someone like you. Tatiana, I'm sure you know, but you are a very pretty woman so niggas will always flirt with you, it doesn't matter who they are."

"When are we going?" I rolled my eyes, making his pretty smile show. I was already in love with it. I'd never been in the presence of a man that was half black and half Asian, but damn were they sexy.

"As soon as I finish eating if that's alright with you. I made the appointment for 9am because I knew ya boy Brevin wouldn't be awake until after noon."

"So you planned your appointment time around me?"

"No, but once he's awake his ass has a pretty tight schedule and he wants Merce and I to be everywhere. Speaking of the devil." He nodded towards his door, and I could hear Merce going into his bedroom next door.

Teflon wiped his hands off with a napkin and then finished his juice. I stood up slowly and rubbed my small bulge as he watched me. He took my hand into his and pulled me closer to him. I couldn't breathe as I waited to find out why he wanted me so close. He placed his hand on my stomach to feel my baby and then stared up into my eyes.

"I don't even know you well, shit not even at all really but strangely

I wish this was mine and not his." *I do too*, I thought.

"Teflon."

"I know, I know. You will learn that I speak my mind all the time. You may hate it at first but it will grow on you."

"Maybe." I stepped back from him so that his hand would fall from being placed on my stomach. I liked the way he touched me way more than a woman involved should have. "So where is this place?"

"Quay."

"Oh, the luxury apartments. Those are nice and only like ten minutes away."

"Are you happy I will still be close?" He was serious, but when I stared deeply into his eyes, he began smiling again. That fucking smile was everything.

"Let's just go."

We left out but I made sure that he didn't come out of the house until ten minutes after me. Brevin may have been asleep but his staff wasn't. They liked me too, but he was the one who signed their checks so that's where their loyalty lied.

Teflon came out about twelve minutes after me and climbed into my car, which I had at the corner of 19th street. Once he got in, I sped off until I was able to get onto the freeway.

It wasn't too hot out, but being away and alone with Teflon made it seem like I was in sweltering heat. Gripping the steering wheel, because my palms felt sweaty, I exhaled heavily to calm my heart rate down. I was nervous for multiple reasons. One was because I was beyond attracted to Teflon and scared of being so close and alone with him, while away from Brevin. Secondly, I was scared of what I might do. I just had to think about my baby.

Teflon's big hand touching my exposed thigh snapped me from my thoughts.

"What are you doing?" I moaned almost.

"We're away from the house Tati, you can chill." He kept his hand sitting on my thigh as if he was my nigga. My clit began to throb feverishly as he swiped his thumb back and forth across my skin. I felt like I was gonna faint. "Relax," he squeezed gently and I swore I came. This was wrong! I was lusting after another man while pregnant.

"I am relaxed," I lied.

We made it to the Quay Apartments in no time and as soon as I found a park, I moved my leg to exit the car. I couldn't stand being under his touch any longer. My leg was even shaking when I got out and tried to stand. He got out on his side and came around to me, grinning like a fool.

"There's the realtor, let's go." He pointed. I nodded and then followed him to the front.

"Good morning, my name is Constance White," she stuck her hand out to shake mine and Teflon's.

"My name is Tre'Wayne German and this is Tatiana." *Tre'Wayne?*

"Nice to meet you both, please follow me."

We followed Constance inside of the building and up to the apartment. It was really nice, but Teflon said he would only be here until he found a house. We were finished about fifteen minutes later and Teflon had decided that he would like to rent the place, but he wanted to talk to Merce before making any moves. She gave us her card after lustfully eyeing him and then we went back to the car. Why was I jealous though?

"Let's go to Gordon," he offered once we were in my car.

"The park?" I frowned.

"Yes the park, I wanna chill but I don't want you to be all nervous and shit like you are at home."

"Teflon someone will see us and they will tell. Brevin owns Cleveland, you know that."

"He doesn't own me and he doesn't run me. The only reason I fall back in front of him is because of you, I couldn't care less if he knows I'm interested in you."

"I'm not this type of person. I don't cheat and I don't sneak around."

"Oh but he can?"

"Yeah, I'm taking you home. Don't try to insult me to get what the fuck you want *Tre'Wayne!*" I spat and he chuckled before placing his hand on top of mine to stop me from cranking the car.

"I wasn't trying to insult you to get my way baby girl. I was only mentioning his ways because I didn't want you to feel guilty about being interested in me."

"Who said I was?"

"Your body told me. When I touch you, your skin gets all hot and shit. The fact that you came with me today and offered to bring me breakfast instead of allowing Suzanne to do it says a lot. Even when I touch your belly, your baby responds positively. And that's big because it's not even mine. Your child is connected to you and feels what you feel."

I just kept shaking my head as he spoke what I knew to be facts. He grabbed my hand into his and kissed the back of it while gazing into my eyes. He was such a beautiful man despite his rugged exterior and thuggish personality.

"Fine," I whispered, taking my hand from him slowly.

I cranked the car and then headed towards the park.

CHAPTER FOUR

Teflon

Once we made it to the park, Tatiana swooped into a space and shut the engine off. I quickly got out and then made my way around to her spot to open the door. Turning my cap to the back, I helped her down, but very slowly and I could almost feel her trembling. It was cute how nervous she got around me and it just proved how really into me she was.

I didn't know what it was about her that had me acting like I wanted to get married in a week and shit. I mean yes she was beautiful, smart, and had a good job and all that shit, but Kayla possessed all of those things as well. Why didn't I feel for Kayla what I felt for Tatiana? I wasn't sure why, but I planned to find out.

Taking Tatiana's hand into mine, I led her to a table near the children's swing set. Since it was a weekday, no kids were there because they were in school. No one was here except a family a few yards away who looked to be having a birthday party for someone. But like I said, I wouldn't have given a fuck if the park was full, I was only being discreet for Tatiana.

We sat next to each other, but I got up because I wanted to sit across from her and stare into her face. Like always, when we held eye contact for too long her attention diverted elsewhere for a couple moments. I took her small hands into mine and examined the small tattoos she had on the inner parts of her wrists.

"You told me you were adopted, do you still talk to your birth mother?" I questioned, watching the wind blow her short curly hair.

"No, not at all. When my parents adopted me, they made sure that my mother agreed to never visit me or anything."

"Damn, have you ever tried looking for her?"

"No, why would I? She didn't want me."

"But there may be a reason why. Maybe she didn't have the means to take care of you at the time, you never know."

"Well if she didn't have the means she shouldn't have been having sex."

"Very true." I chuckled at how cute her twisted up face was. "Can I ask you something? And you must promise me that you won't get mad and you will just answer."

"Fine."

"Why are you with Brevin?"

"Because I love him, Teflon. Why else would I be with him? I love him. We've been together for years… I love him."

"You're saying it so many times that now I'm wondering who exactly you're trying to convince baby."

"I'm not trying to convince anyone or anything, it's a fact."

"Okay." I nodded.

"What do you mean okay?" her frown was deeply embedded into her face.

"I mean okay. I asked you a question and you answered it for me."

"Where is your girlfriend? I'm sure you have one somewhere, maybe in California."

"I did have a girlfriend before I moved here named Kayla, but we ended things before I left. I'm not tied to anything Tatiana."

"Why did you say that last part? It wouldn't matter to me if you were tied down or not." She sucked her teeth and rolled her eyes. It was the first time I'd ever seen her give any attitude like that. It was kind of cute.

"You care, but I won't go there. I'm not gonna force you to express your feelings. You'll do it when you're ready, hopefully."

There was silence as she glanced from my eyes to the rest of the park. I on the other hand kept my attention on her pretty face, well her side profile.

"Who named you Tre'Wayne?" she smiled, turning her attention back to me.

"My mother. My dad was a big time cheater, so she didn't want to name any of her kids after him. She named me after some guy she got friendly with while my dad was away for months with one of his mistresses. She swears she and the guy were just friends, but I'm not sure how true that is."

"Interesting background." She nodded as the wind blew through her hair. "You have any siblings?"

"A little brother named Thomas who is studying abroad right now, but attends Cleveland State. I have an older brother Torrey who is locked up, not terrorizing the streets of Cleveland at the moment."

Tired of being so far away, I got up and came around the table to sit next to her. She blinked a couple of times like always, letting me know she was a little bit uncomfortable, but I didn't care. She would get over that shit. I placed her hands into mine and intertwined our fingers as we both looked down at our hands clasped together.

"I don't even know you," she whispered.

"Where did that come from?"

She sighed before saying, "I don't even know you, yet holding your hand feels right. And like you said before when you touch my baby…"

She was right. I felt a closeness with her, something I should have felt with Kayla. I hadn't even gave her this dick yet, but somehow I was developing feelings for her. A nigga hadn't been back in Cleveland for a damn month and shit was already popping off. I really liked shorty, but more importantly, I wanted her and those were two totally different things.

Liking her was something I could handle and do from afar, but wanting her meant that I would have to step into uncharted territory. As much as I felt like Brevin was a fuck nigga, I worked for him and she was his girl. I had no idea how this would play out, but I wasn't about to walk away without Tatiana on my arm.

I turned her body to face mine and then snaked my arms around her torso. Pulling her in, I hugged her small frame tightly as I inhaled her scent. She smelled like brown sugar and lavender or some shit like that. I had become familiar with the smell since staying in Brevin's home. Intrigued by the feel of her soft skin and the smell of her body and hair, I kissed the area where her neck met her shoulder.

"Teflon," she whispered my name without any words to follow it like she always did.

I trailed my lips from her shoulder to the side of her neck, eventually landing on her ear. Her small hands were gripping my biceps as I hugged her body as if I never wanted to let it go. Sucking on her ear, I let my tongue go in and then brought my lips to the front of her neck and eventually her collarbone. I kept away from her lips, because for some reason I wanted to save those.

"Let me go," she finally said, slightly nudging me.

I did as she asked, but not right away, because I didn't want to. I kissed her cheek and then got up to go around the table to look into her face again. We continued to talk about all kinds of shit like nothing had just happened, before we realized it was starting to get dark.

"Wanna get some food?"

"It's already getting dark, Teflon. Brevin has probably been calling us both."

"Let's just get some food and then we can head home."

"Fine." She gave me a closed mouth smile.

CHAPTER FOUR

Tatiana

"I'll drive you," Teflon held his hand out for my car keys as we trucked it through the park. I didn't like niggas driving my car, but right now I didn't mind. And I could tell that at the moment, I didn't have an option. Digging into my purse, I retrieved my keys and placed them into the palm of his hand.

We drove to this place named Momocho, which was a Mexican food restaurant. I told him that was what I was in the mood for and he claimed this place was the business as he put it. I was starving right now and didn't really care where we went as long as I could get some taquitos and he claimed they had the best ones.

After parking my car, he got out and jogged around to open the door for me and help me out. I glanced around a bit to see if anybody I knew was hanging around, but I noticed nothing. And Brevin knew a gang of niggas that I didn't, so it may very well be someone out here willing to snitch, I just didn't recognize them.

"Chill out, you good," Teflon said, closing the car door behind me.

"I am chill, you chill." I smirked. I was getting more comfortable with him than I was before and I liked that. Despite his rugged exterior and brash demeanor, he was pretty cool, laid back, and chill.

The restaurant had a nice amount of people, but it wasn't as crowded as it would be if it were the weekend. We were seated almost immediately, and although I knew what I wanted, I scanned over the menu for a few minutes before closing it.

"Have you decided already, baby girl?" I loved that he called me that, but I would continue to pretend to despise any pet name he assigned to me.

"Yes, I want the taquitos remember?"

"Oh yeah." He chuckled. "I think I'm gonna get that too." He closed the menu and then clasped his hands together. When he did that, his muscles bulged and I got a little throb down below.

"Why did your girlfriend break up with you?" I asked, just as a waitress approached our table. We gave her our food and beverage orders and then stayed silent until she walked away. As soon as she left though I turned my attention right back to Teflon, making his alluring smile appear.

"How the fuck you know she was the one to break up with me?"

"Well for one I can tell because of how hard you're grinning, and secondly I doubt she would do something to jeopardize a relationship with you."

"I wasn't the most faithful nigga." My smile faded, because I'd come back to reality and realized the whole fairytale I'd drawn up in my head was never gonna come true with a nigga like Teflon. "And so she decided it would be best to end things."

"Did you beg?"

"Not this time no, because I felt like it was best for us to be apart for now." *For now,* I repeated in my head.

"Oh so once you get yourself together you're going back to get her?"

The waitress came to set our drinks down and once she sauntered off he said, "No. I'm hoping to get into something else here in Cleveland." His gaze was intense and locked on me, causing goosebumps to appear all over my arms.

"Well good luck," I half smiled.

After talking for about thirty more minutes, our food arrived and we scarfed it down. I even ate some of his, which he didn't seem to mind at all. After our dinner, we went to Mitchell's for some ice cream and by that time, it was completely dark outside.

"I'm gonna turn my phone on now." I smiled as he drove us home, before holding down the power button on my iPhone.

"Turn mine on too." He removed it from his pocket and placed it in my lap.

Staring down at his iPhone turned off, I finally picked it up and powered it on like he'd requested. My heart rate sped up as I waited for the screen to light up. Mine was buzzing and chiming away in my lap, but I was focused on Teflon's. Finally, his was awake and a plethora of texts and missed calls came in from Merce, Brevin, his ex Kayla, unknown numbers, and about three other females that I was sure he'd smashed while in a relationship.

"Here you go." I placed the phone into the cup holder and then picked mine up. I could feel him looking at me, but I kept my attention on my phone.

Jadynn: Breakfast tomorrow? I have to talk to you.

Me: Okay.

Cecily: Don't forget about your nail appointment!

Me: I haven't forgotten, goodnight.

Brevin: Where the fuck are you? You got me fucked up on everything I love Tatiana!!!! You better hope I'm sleep when you walk through this door!

I swallowed the lump in my throat after reading Brevin's text. I was scared out of my mind because I knew he wasn't playing and I was sure that his ass was twisted. My breathing became heavy as Teflon pulled up to the curb in front of Brevin's and my mansion. He shut the engine off and then touched my exposed thigh again.

"Stop!" I smacked his hand away, prompting a confused expression to cover his face.

"What did that nigga say?"

"Nothing. I will go in and you come in after me. Remember to wait ten minutes!" I spat and then hopped out of the car, not caring about what the fuck he had to say and not caring that he had my car keys. I was too on edge to think clearly.

I entered the house slowly and then made my way upstairs to the bedroom I shared with Brevin. I prayed that the text he'd sent was from a while ago, because I didn't want to get into it with his crazy ass. When I opened the bedroom door, I let out a sigh of relief when I saw the room was empty. He was probably with another bitch, but right now I was happy about that.

I went into the bathroom and undressed for a hot shower, and once I was clean, I brushed my teeth, and put on a nightshirt. I then covered myself in body butter, and braided up my hair, before walking out into the bedroom. My stomach dropped when I spotted Brevin standing there with his fists balled up.

"Where the fuck have you been all day?"

"At work, Brevin—"

WHAM!

He slapped me so hard that I fell onto the nearby chair and hit my forehead.

"You couldn't answer your fucking phone all day? And you expect me to believe you were working? Since when do you ignore me Tatiana?" he spoke, spit was flying everywhere as he slapped me and pulled on my hair. "Get up!" he barked and I stood up from the floor, while trying to dab at the blood that was coming from my nose.

"Brevin stop! I forgot to charge my phone and it died while—"

WHAM!

This time he punched me and I flew into the wall. He yanked me up by neck with one hand and then reached under my nightshirt with his other hand to rip my panties. I tried pushing and scratching, but I was no match for him whatsoever. He pushed his sweats and boxers down just enough to release himself and then rammed into me forcefully. He continued fucking me roughly up against the wall as he squeezed my neck tightly. I could smell the other bitch's perfume on him as he continued to have his way with me.

Suddenly the door burst open and Brevin was shoved to the side and punched so ferociously that I felt his blood splatter on my neck. I dropped to the floor as Teflon whooped Brevin's ass right in front of me. He punched and punched, and the more he ravaged Brevin, the more blood I saw.

"Tef! Man calm down before you kill the nigga!" Merce came in and pulled Teflon off Brevin.

"Fuck out of my house!" Brevin hollered as he hopped to his feet and stumbled back a little bit, fixing his pants. "When I come back be gone!" he shouted. Teflon tried to charge him again, but Merce and eventually Groove had to stop him. Brevin just rushed out and then Groove looked down at me in horror.

I felt liquid between my legs and began to panic as I witnessed a pool of blood forming from my center.

"No!" I cried and screamed as Groove helped me up from the floor. "My baby!"

"Call 911!" Teflon hollered as he assisted Groove in helping me up. He eventually picked me up bridal style.

"Nigga you're getting blood all over you!" Groove hollered as Merce spoke with the 911 agent.

"I don't give a fuck! Tell them niggas to hurry the fuck up, Merce!" Teflon screamed so loudly that I felt the vibration coming from his chest.

I buried my face into him as I sobbed uncontrollably, and I felt his lips against my forehead. Just as the sounds of sirens were heard and Teflon was carrying me down the stairs, I passed out.

***

I opened my eyes and blinked a few times. I heard the beeping of hospital machines, so I knew where I was. The memory of what happened to me flooded my mind immediately, causing tears to well up in my eyes. I heard movement to my left and knew it was Brevin's crazy ass. Turning my attention to him, I was surprised to see it was Teflon. Why was he here? Brevin was supposed to be here.

Teflon saw that I was awake, so he stood up, adjusting himself in his gray sweats. His tattooed and muscular chest, abs, and arms looked so good under his wife beater. He was so damn sexy that it was a shame. After slipping his socked feet into his Nike slide ins, he made his way closer to the bed.

"How are you feeling?"

My stomach felt weird so I asked, "The baby, is it—" I was cut off when he shook his head 'no'. His thumb brushed against my cheek as I closed my eyes to hold back some of my tears. I couldn't help it though so I eventually broke down. I didn't even know why I'd asked. I could never forget delivering my dead baby.

"Baby girl don't—" He sucked his teeth and then leaned down to wrap me in his strong arms. "Relax, baby."

"Where is he?" I sobbed, resisting the hug he was attempting to give to me. I could see the disappointment in his face at the fact that I

111

was asking for Brevin. It wasn't that I missed him, it was that he should want to be here knowing I miscarried yet again.

"After he stormed out he hasn't been back, but Merce is trying to find him," he finally answered, pursing his lips together. He pulled me back into his chest and every time I inhaled sharply while sobbing, I smelled his cologne. I loved that it wasn't too much, just the right amount of sexy.

He held me tightly until my crying ceased and I fell back asleep. Brevin was supposed to be here.

CHAPTER FIVE

Brevin

The next morning…

woke up feeling terrible as hell. Not really because of what happened the night before, but because I drank myself into oblivion and my head was pounding. I was starting to feel like I was developing a bit of a problem because I could barely make it through the day without polishing a bottle off.

I placed both of my hands on my face, massaging my eyes, hoping to ease the tension I felt at the bridge of my nose. Once the pain started to subside a little, last night's events invaded my mind. All I remembered was manhandling Tatiana and then getting fucked up by that nigga Teflon. I was already drunk off my ass and I'd done a line or two as well, so half of the shit I did was a blur. Suddenly visions of a crying and screaming Tatiana entered my mind, making me sit up.

Believe it or not I loved that girl, but she pissed me off constantly with her bullshit. She needed to know her place as the woman of a kingpin and realize there was shit she couldn't do and shit I could. I could stay out all night and I could entertain the opposite sex, but she couldn't. I still didn't even know where the hell she'd been all day and when I asked my staff around the house, they said she'd left alone.

Funny enough that nigga Teflon was missing in action around the same time as her, but I knew deep down she would never fuck with a nigga like him. Tatiana tried to play the good girl role, but she was into niggas with fat pockets. And although Teflon wasn't broke by any means, he wasn't getting the type of bread that I was, therefore he couldn't bag the type of bitches I could.

"You're finally up. Are you hungry?" This girl named Amanda walked into the bedroom. I'd been fucking Amanda off and on for a minute now, so when I rushed out last night I came straight here.

"Yeah what you got?" I sat up and swung my feet off the side of the bed.

"I made pancakes, eggs, sausage, and I cut up some fruit. I will bring it to you," she replied and I nodded as I stared down at her carpet.

Grabbing my phone from the dresser, I saw I had some texts from Groove, Merce, and Mack. I expected one from that bitch ass nigga Teflon, apologizing to me at the least, but there was nothing of the sort.

Groove: *Nigga where are you? The baby was stillborn.*

My chest tightened as I read what Groove texted to me. This would be the second baby that we lost and despite how I came off that shit hurt like hell. I had plans for that kid and Tatiana and I had even chosen a name. I blamed myself and at this point, I was too ashamed to face Tatiana and anyone else that was in the house last night.

"Here." Amanda walked in with a tray of food and slid it into my lap. "Why so glum, baby?"

"Yo, back up. I don't like people that close to me while I'm eating and shit, Mandy."

"Sorry." She scooted over some. "But why are you looking so depressed?"

"My fiancée lost the baby," I mumbled damn near, as I shoved some pancakes into my mouth. I didn't even have an appetite anymore.

"Again?" She sucked her teeth as if it were Tatiana's fault.

"Fuck you sucking your teeth for?"

"Calm down, Brevin, I'm just surprised that she lost this one when she was so far along. You usually don't lose it that late. But don't get mad at me baby, I'm on your side. You know I want whatever makes you happy."

"Show me," I said placing the tray of food to the side. Maybe some of her A1 head game would help me get my mind off losing my kid.

Amanda happily dropped to her knees and removed my dick from my boxers. As soon as she started sucking the tip, I got even harder than I was before. Amanda didn't have the best body, because she was hella skinny, but I wasn't tripping. Shit, Tatiana barely had any titties, so I wasn't gonna complain about Amanda, who funny enough had some knockers.

"Damn," I mumbled as my head bumped the back of her throat while she snaked her tongue around my shaft. This bitch had a degree in dick sucking. "Shit!" I grumbled when I looked to see Mack was calling me. "What's good?"

"Where you at, Brev?"

"I'm busy— Aye, I'm at Amanda's. I need you to drop by my house and get me some clothes and shit. Get me a lot of stuff."

"Nigga, I don't know what you want me to bring and who the hell is Amanda?"

"Some girl— fuck baby, just like that." I looked down at her slurping my dick up like she had something to prove. Shit, prove it baby. Prove it.

"Nigga, what the hell are you doing over there?" Mack barked.

"Chill man. Look, just bring me some boxers, sweats, a t-shirt, my chains, and my watch. Oh and get my soap and toothbrush. I will shop for some more shit later. Fuck shorty… damn."

"Gloria is with me, is that cool?"

"Yeah." I hung up and then used that hand to guide Amanda's head up and down my dick. A few minutes later, I was spilling into her mouth and feeling one hundred times better.

"Better?" she licked her lips and stood to her feet.

I just nodded in response and grabbed the tray of food to polish it off since I was feeling a little famished now.

About forty-five minutes later, Mack and Gloria showed up with the shit I asked for. I took a shower, brushed my teeth, and then got dressed in what he'd brought from my house. When I was done, I entered the living room where the three of them sat in silence.

"Why you ain't going home?" Mack quizzed with a confused

expression, glancing from Amanda to me.

"Some shit popped off with Tatiana and that new nigga I hired, Teflon." I plopped down onto the couch.

"What he do?"

"Tatiana and I were talking and he came in trying to save her ass, hitting me and shit. I fired his bitch ass so I hope he has luck finding work in my city."

"Well we have a couple meetings to hit up and shit Brevin, so let's go."

"Nah I'm not really in the mood right now, Mack. You can go meet with everybody and tell them I'm on a little break right now."

"Why nigga th—"

"Come outside." I cut him off and rose to my feet.

Once we got in the backyard, I closed the door behind his stupid ass. "Tatiana lost the baby and I'm not in the mood to deal with any damn body. I just wanna relax and get that shit off of my mind for a few days."

"Where is she?"

"The hospital I'm sure."

"Damn, wanna go see her—"

"Nah I don't. This happened before so she doesn't really need my support like that. She knows what the hell to do. For now, I'm just gonna lay low here."

"Brev man, I don't think that's a—"

"Did I ask you what you thought was a good idea, nigga?" I stepped closer to him.

Sometimes Mack got out of line and forgot who the fuck was in charge. I didn't need him telling me how to handle my situation, especially one that I'd experienced before. I wasn't in the mood to see Tatiana act all sad and shit, moping around the fucking house like she needed to be on suicide watch. And what about me? It was my kid too. I just needed some time away from all that shit.

"I feel you."

As soon as those words left his mouth, we heard Gloria and Amanda arguing. Mack and I rushed back inside to see them hella close to throwing hands.

"I don't know why you care who Brevin is fucking!" Amanda hollered.

"You're a fucking hoe! But let me show you why I care!" Gloria started towards Amanda but I put Amanda behind me.

"Mack, get yo' girl and bounce. Take care of that meeting shit too and don't bring her along."

I knew it had to be an ego bruiser to see his bitch fighting over me. I mean she didn't come out of her mouth and say why she was mad, but it was obvious she wasn't fucking with the idea of me laying up with Amanda. She had her damn nerve though.

"Chill, Amanda, ignore her ass," I barked after closing and locking the door behind Gloria and Mack.

"Why does she care who you fuck? Are you fucking your

homeboy's girl?"

"My business is mine and yours is yours. Don't worry about who I'm fucking when I'm here with you. All you need to be doing is cherishing the fucking time we have together."

"I know. I just get jealous easily."

"Well don't, that's not your place at the moment. I have a fiancée, remember?" She nodded her head slowly before looking off. "Straight up Amanda, if Tatiana wasn't around, I'd be about you." I lied like a muthafucka!

I pressed my lips against hers, which usually I would never do. The only reason I was buttering her up like this was because I wanted her to let me stay here for a bit. I knew it was unlikely that she'd kick me out, because she was desperate for my time, but I wasn't in the mood for any surprises.

I planned to lay low for as long as I needed though, maybe a week, so why not get some good pussy and home cooked meals without the commitment while doing so.

CHAPTER FIVE

Jadynn

Two weeks later…

I really didn't even know why I was so sad about Russell cheating on me. I think I was more upset that it was with my sister, someone who was supposed to have my fucking back. And with all the shit she talked about him you'd think she'd be the last person on earth in his bed, but I guess she was just trying to make me leave him alone.

I will admit that it worked a little bit because at times she would be able to get in my head. Sometimes after talking with her, I would tell myself that as soon as I saw him I would sit him down and tell him it was over. I was never able to once he and I came face to face though.

I blew out hot air as I slipped my blazer over my back. This shit combined with Brevin killing his and Tatiana's baby was too much for me. She was so sad and depressed every time I went to visit her in the hospital. I swear I wanted to whoop his ass, but he was nowhere to be found right now. What a perfect time to disappear right? Just when your fiancée needs you the most. Surprisingly, that dude Teflon had been with her everyday like he was her nigga and that was his baby. Even though he wasn't the father and he wasn't Brevin, I think both Tatiana and I found a sense of relief in the fact that he was with her a lot.

We both needed just to move the fuck on though, because it was long overdue. Russell and Brevin weren't shit and were never gonna be shit.

I heard someone knocking at my door like they were the police, so after sliding my feet into my shoes, I rushed over. It must have been my mom, because she was the only one who would be popping up at this time. Paige wouldn't dare and neither would Russell and since Tatiana was in the hospital recovering still, my mom was the only option.

Looking through the peephole, my face immediately twisted up at the sight of this asshole. Yanking my door open, I slapped the shit out of him before either of us could say a word.

Nodding his head with his tongue in his cheek, Russell rubbed the area that I'd slapped. I wanted to go upside his fucking head again, but then I thought… for what? I didn't want this nigga whatsoever. Why should I get all sweaty and tired whooping his ass? I just needed to take my ass to work, because now that Tatiana had been out of commission for the past two weeks, my workload seemed to quadruple.

"I deserve that," he finally said, slipping his hands into the pocket of his hoodie.

"Obviously. What the fuck are you doing at my door?"

"I came to get my stuff; why else would I be here? I mean I was gonna apologize and shit, but you putting ya hands on me changed my mind."

"Well as far as you picking up your *shit,* I gave it Goodwill. They gave me a nice amount of money for the *shit* too. Maybe if you get there fast enough, they'll be able to sell it back to you."

The fire in his eyes was enough to light a furnace for a full Christmas season. I didn't care though, because most of the shit he had I bought, so it was my right to get the money for it. Paige made more than enough money to replenish his damn wardrobe though, so he'd better hop to it and see if he could get his shit back for a price, or hit her up for her card.

"This is exactly why I went for your damn sister and stopped fucking with you!" He barged into my spot, shoulder checking me with his big ass.

"Nah nigga, you need to get the fuck out!" I shouted loudly, hoping a neighbor or some shit would hear me and call the police, because I damn sure didn't have the strength to put him out.

He walked up to me, slammed the door, and then rushed me into the wall. I'd never been scared of Russell before, but right now I was frightened as hell. I mean he was a bitch ass nigga, but he didn't look like one at all. He was tall, muscular, and had dark scary eyes. You wouldn't know he was a mark ass bitch until you got to know him.

"Move Russell," I spoke in a calmer tone, hoping to ease the tension between us.

"Either you get my shit from Goodwill, or give me the money they gave you," he gritted, barely allowing his rows of teeth to separate from one another as he spoke.

"Fuck you—"

He choked me up the wall and shook me like a rag doll as his face twisted up even more.

"I'm tired of yo' fucking mouth, Jadynn! This is exactly why I cheated on you! You talk too fucking much and you ain't about shit! All you do is work, hang out with Tatiana, and talk shit! You gon' stop treating me like a bitch!" He gripped my neck.

"Russ— Russell," I managed to say before he tightened his grip.

"Say sorry."

"No," I whispered.

WHAM!

He let my neck go and backhanded me like some whore. Flying to the floor, I burned my knee once it scraped against the carpet. Blood dripped from my nose onto the floor as I gripped my knee hoping to ease the pain. Before I could do or say anything, he slapped my again, making me fly onto my back. Climbing on top of me, he reached under my skirt and ripped my panties.

"You gon' respect me," he growled, forcing my legs apart.

"Russell, no! Stop!" I tried to fight him but he was using all the strength he had to pin me down. Two of my wrists fit into his one hand as he pushed his sweats down to reveal his dick. "Stop! Please Russell! I'm sorry!" I cried, hoping he'd accept my apology. "Ah!" I screamed once he entered me.

"Look at you now. You ain't so bad are you?" He grinned evilly as he pumped in out of me.

"Ow!" I yelled when he bit down on my lip, drawing blood.

He ripped my blouse with his free hand and rubbed all over the exposed areas of my skin as he humped me like a rabid dog.

"Mmm," he grumbled as he released a warm substance into my body. The rape was a quick five minutes, but it seemed like it'd lasted forever.

He finally caught his breath and slid out of me. Wiping the spit from his mouth with the back of his hand, he stood to his feet and looked around the room. He spotted my purse and put his dick away before walking over to it. I laid there in shock, crying because I couldn't believe how my life had changed in only a matter of weeks.

"Thanks." He chuckled, counting the little bit of cash he'd removed from my wallet. "For the money and the pussy. I hate everything about you but that pussy was always good."

After grabbing a bottled water from the fridge, he left my condo.

I just laid there, sobbing and sore, wondering what I ever did to deserve some shit like this.

I Got Your Back ◆ *Teflon & Tatiana's Love Story*

CHAPTER FIVE

Teflon

A couple weeks later...

"Teflon this is way too nice," Tatiana sighed as we entered the hotel room I booked for us.

She was finally out of the hospital and feeling a little better I assume. That nigga Brevin hadn't come to see her once and I was hoping he did. She'd been in the damn hospital for three and a half weeks and he didn't show up at all. He didn't even send flowers. I wanted him to show up, not because he needed to, but because I wanted to finish giving him that ass whooping he'd earned.

That shit that he did to her had me hot and the fact that she lost her baby had me feeling some type of way too because I knew it was the second time. The kid wasn't mine, but for some reason I felt like he and I had some sort of connection. Yeah, we found out it was boy. I shook my head as I set her bag down.

We'd been by the house to pack her some things because I told her she wasn't staying with that nigga anymore. I could see in her eyes that she wanted to see him and it bothered me. Why did that shit bother me? I really didn't know. I guess it was because I wanted her and knowing she wanted him, even though he didn't deserve her made me sick to my fucking stomach.

I had bitches I had to block because they wouldn't leave me alone, yet here I was yearning for a woman who barely showed any interest in me. I mean we flirted and I knew she liked me, but I wasn't sure if she thought about me daily like I did her. I hadn't even been back in Cleveland that long and she had me feeling like this. I hadn't even felt this way about Kayla, a woman I spent years with.

"It's not too much. It's a nice spot. You hungry? We can order room service."

"No, I'd just like to lie down."

She stood in the middle of the room, admiring it still. She was so beautiful, captivating almost. Her small frame was sexy despite the fact that she didn't have the assets I typically went for and her skin looked so supple. Her eyes were regular brown, but they were more beautiful to me than other people's. She had her short curly hair hanging down, and her full lips poked out a little, as she removed her tights. I watched with my mouth partially open and just like that my dick was hard from seeing her smooth legs.

"Baby," I walked over to her and kneeled down just as she sat on the bed. She let me stay near her and I took that chance to get a glance between her legs. I know, she'd just miscarried and it should have been the last thing I was thinking about but I couldn't help it. I'd been fantasizing about smashing her for the longest. "What can I do to cheer your pretty ass up?" I smirked, rubbing my hands up and down the sides of her small thighs.

Everything about her was small besides her big brown eyes and big lips, but it still turned me on. And I was a nigga who loved coke bottle shaped bitches all day and wouldn't even look your way if them titties were little.

"I'm okay, Tef. I promise," she smiled, brightening up the room almost. Reaching up under the big t-shirt she had on, I touched her stomach, which was still bulging a bit, but not nearly as much as it was before obviously. "The doctor says it'll go away in no time. My body is getting back to normal…" She placed her hand on top of mine.

"I was wondering what the fuck was going on." We laughed in unison, but her smile quickly faded and a tear traveled down her cheek.

"How long are we gonna be here?"

"Just until I move into that apartment."

"The one by the water? You already put in an offer?"

"Yeah, Merce and I scored two spots in the building. I did everything while you were in the hospital, and I get the keys in a couple of days after filling out some paperwork."

"I can't move with you, Teflon."

"Why not?"

"Because, I… I don't want you to get the wrong idea." She stood up.

"What wrong idea?"

"That I'm gonna leave Brevin and that you and I are gonna be in some kind of relationship or that you're gonna be sleeping with me."

"Wow!"

"Don't act like that's not what you wanted."

I took my shirt off because I was about to shower as I let what she was saying to me sink in. I had to chuckle even.

"Yeah it was what I wanted when I thought you were something other than what the fuck I'm seeing now. That nigga whooped yo' ass and killed your fucking child, yet you still wanna be with him?" I frowned. More tears spilled down her cheeks, but she just quickly wiped them like it meant nothing.

"It's not that simple. He and I are getting married and I've been with him for a long time, Teflon! You can't just come into my life and disrupt things! And I can't just drop everything with him because he and I have a problem!"

"Noted." I headed towards the bathroom.

Tatiana was someone that I wanted, but I couldn't stand a weak bitch. If she wanted to stick with that nigga while he cheated on her, whooped her ass, and killed every baby that they conceived that was fine with me. Shit… I plopped down on the closed toilet top and exhaled sharply at my thoughts. I was lying like fuck. There was no way I was gonna just turn my back on her situation. Why did I feel so invested when I didn't know her from a can of paint? My body ached at the thought of letting her go and leaving her with that nigga. She had a nigga thinking that she was my soul mate or some shit. It's almost like I was brought back here to Ohio to meet her.

Shaking my head, I stood up and turned the shower on. As the warm water poured down over me, I tried to get Tatiana out of my mind. I needed to sever any attachment I had to her right now, so that over time it would only get easier being away from her.

I cut the water off and wrapped a towel around myself before exiting the bathroom. The lights were off and she was in the bed sleep. I slipped some new boxers on, before sitting down and pulling my burner phone out.

Merce: I finally found this nigga. It's been three weeks and some change. The streets have been dry and every damn thing.

I'd given up on looking for Brevin, because honestly Tatiana was the only thing on my mind. I knew the streets were drying up because he wasn't working, but again, baby girl had consumed my mind and I didn't really care about that shit either.

Me: Word where?

Merce: Some bitch's crib that think she's his shorty. Crazy.

Merce: How is Tatiana?

Me: Better. Got out today, but I'm ready to drop her ass of at his crib.

Merce: Nah.

Me: Yeah, she wants to be near him so I'm gonna let her.

Me: I can't work for homie no more, Merce.

Merce: Me either. If I had enough ammo I would have taken care of him.

Me: Man… It's time to find a new hustle though.

***Merce:** Yup.*

I removed the SIM card from the phone and set it on the computer desk in the room. I then got up to check and see if there were some covers in the closet that I could use to lie down in that fucking chair. I didn't even wanna be next to her right now.

"Tef," her sweet voice whispered, waking my dick up.

"Sup," I responded without looking her way, continuing to sift through the bullshit in the closet. I knew nothing was in there by this time, but still.

"What are you looking for?"

"I'm looking for a blanket."

"Why? You can sleep in the bed." She sighed.

I paused, inhaling, before I closed the closet door and walked over. Peeling the covers back, I climbed into the bed, and turned my back to her. I couldn't look at her pretty ass or she would reel me back in.

"Look tomorrow I will take you home. Merce found your nigga at…" I decided not to finish because for some odd ass fucking reason I didn't want her knowing that while she was laid up in the hospital, her nigga was up under another bitch.

"Okay," she said so lowly, that I almost couldn't make it out. I could hear the sadness in her voice, which was surprising considering the fact that her ass *wanted* to go home.

I fluffed my pillow and laid down, ignoring her sad demeanor. I couldn't do this shit with her. She had me acting out of character in less than a damn month, and what was it for? So she could use me to satisfy her emotional needs. My face frowned although my eyes were closed, proving that I wouldn't sleep easily tonight.

After a few minutes I heard a little bit of movement and then felt her soft hands on my back, rubbing the big ass cross tattooed on it. She then put her soft ass lips against me and that easily I was rock solid below the waist. Turning to face her, I realized she'd taken her big t-shirt off, and she didn't have any underwear on.

Almost as if it were a reflex, I crushed my lips against hers while climbing on top of her and getting in between her legs. Her lips were like silk pillows or soft cotton. I couldn't get enough of sucking them and biting them as I groped her small frame. A nigga felt like he'd never been intimate with a woman before. I think because I'd been dreaming about this shit for the longest.

After kissing her so hard that her lips turned red and letting my tongue dance with hers for an eternity it seemed, I trailed my kisses to her neck. Her skin was so soft under me like pound cake.

"Can you do this?" I questioned. I didn't know anyone who had miscarried so I wasn't sure when she could have sex.

"Yeah, the nurse said it was fine. The bleeding has stopped and stuff." She nodded, rubbing her little hands up and down my big bicep. "It was almost a month ago Teflon, it's fine."

I grabbed the hand she caressed me with and kissed from the palm of it down to her neck. I then cupped her small breasts as much as they would allow and sucked her nipples hungrily. Everything about this girl was perfect. Her imperfections were even flawless. The shit I thought I wanted in a woman didn't even matter to me when it came to Tatiana.

After getting my fix with her nipples, I continued down until I reached her slightly bulging midsection. She tensed up, and tugged my hair a little to stop me.

"You don't have to. I know it feels weird." She half smiled, but I knew she was uncomfortable.

"Do you know how sexy you are?" I furrowed my brows. She didn't smile or say anything. Her mouth stayed in an O shape as she looked down at me with her big brown eyes. "Let me take care of you."

I lightly kissed her smooth stomach, running my hand down it when I was done, before making it to her love box. I got comfortable, squeezing her butt and pushing her pussy closer into my face. She placed her legs over my shoulders, rubbing my hair as she waited. We made eye contact as I planted soft kisses on her middle, inhaling the natural scent it carried. Her moans were just as sexy as I had expected soft, sweet, and soothing.

Taking her clit into my mouth, I sucked it gently while staring up at her. Her beautiful face was balled up, as she ran her small hand through her thick, shoulder length, curly brown hair. Her chest rose and fell, with her nipples hard, and sweat running between her breasts. She had a mole like Marilyn Monroe under one of them, which I found to also be sexy. What wasn't sexy about her?

"Tre…" she moaned part of my government name, while gripping my hair in her hands.

Her little frame trembled, releasing her juices into my mouth.

I licked them up instantly and kept sucking her clit feverishly. Her breathing became shallow as I sucked on her pussy like a fucking lollipop. A nigga had been dreaming about this box and I was gonna savor the moment.

Pushing one of her legs towards her stomach by her thigh, I pressed my face further into it. Her moans became high-pitched whimpers and her breathing could now be heard along with it. That only motivated me and by the time she exploded she was damn near crying.

"Mmm," she cooed, biting down on her lip and shivering a little bit.

I kissed back up her beautiful body until I was at her lips. Our tongues immediately came in contact and we got right to kissing nastily. My dick had never been this hard ever. I felt her soft thighs against the sides of my body as I lied between her legs, tonguing her down and groping her.

"I want you so bad," I whispered never allowing her lips to leave mine.

She had her arms draped around my neck and her ankles crossed, locking me in. I pushed my boxers down and found a way to get them off without taking my lips from hers. My rod seemed to be knocking at her opening on its own and damn was she wet. I pressed one of her legs into her stomach and we both watched as I tried to enter her. She resisted me, but I pushed harder until I had the head in.

"Fuck Tati!" I groaned against her lips. I had no business fucking this girl raw, but she had me in my fucking feelings and her pussy was already feeling too good, pulling me in and shit.

"Uhh!" She let out that sweet sexy whimper, as I pushed myself further into her super tight hole. "Tef," she cried, as I moved in and out of her slowly, getting her used to my girth.

"Yo," I growled to myself, trying to calm my dick down. This shit was really happening and her pussy felt just as good as I thought, even better.

She locked her ankles again, which made her legs spread wider and finally I had my movement down since her pussy was accepting me. We resumed kissing as I pounded her slowly, moaning every time I got all the way in. I didn't moan during sex usually, not until a few seconds before cumming, but she had me.

"Mmm, aaah, aahh!" Her voice quivered as if she were about to cry every time she hit the base of my dick. This was too much and I wasn't sure how much longer I could last.

Feeling her small hands grip my biceps, which she could barely do, I bit down on her lip before pushing my tongue back into her mouth. I wound my hips into her, sitting inside for a few seconds, and then sliding out slowly. Her body shook as she coated my dick. Lord, help me stay strong.

Lifting myself up so that my palms were flat against the bed, I rammed her pussy like it was going out of style until she came again. I then lowered myself back onto her and began tonguing her down while beating it up. She yelled into my mouth, while digging her nails into my ribcage, and I didn't slow up until I was close to cumming. When I was ready, I pulled out, snatched some tissues from the box on the nightstand, and set them down between her legs. I started to jack myself off, but she moved my hand and did it for me, sucking on the tip a little bit. This girl man…

"I'm about to nut, fuck." I threw my head back, enjoying the feeling of her small hands and warm wet mouth. When she felt my dick get brick hard, she let go, and I came on the tissue, growling like a damn forest animal. I had never cum that hard in all of my twenty-eight years. As I panted, trying to catch my breath, she rubbed and pecked my six-pack lightly.

I cleaned up the tissue and then got some towels for us to wipe with. Once we were done, we laid down together, her head on my chest and her small leg draped across my lower half. I ran my fingers through her shoulder length curly hair, as we laid there in silence, still breathing a little hard.

With the way she liked to play games with me, this was a bad idea. She had me acting like a straight up female.

CHAPTER FIVE

Tatiana

You'd think that I'd be feeling guilty for sleeping with Teflon, but I felt relaxed as if it were normal. There was no voice in my head telling me stop, or any bad feelings washing over me. And the way he looked at me, the way he made my body feel, I didn't understand. I didn't get why God had me in a relationship with Brevin for so long and not with Teflon instead. The way we'd just made love was how it was supposed to be with Brevin. The way he doted on me, the way he did everything that my fiancé was supposed to do. A part of me wanted to sleep with him again, but my vagina was still sore and I guess it'd been through a lot.

"I've only been with Brevin," I whispered with my eyes closed. I loved when people touched my hair and Teflon was running his fingers through it at the moment. The room was dark, but we could see enough.

"Sexually?" he quizzed in his calm voice. I loved his voice. It was raspy and deep, yet soothing.

"Yes. I never thought I would want to do it with anyone else."

"I feel special then." He chuckled. His body was so fucking ripped, almost like he'd come out of a magazine. He was so tall and muscular and I was so small. It was funny. "Did you like it?"

"Yes, too much." He looked down at me and kissed the scars on my face that Brevin put there. I kept my eyes closed because his lips felt good against them.

"I ain't pushing you to do anything because you don't know me and like you said, it ain't cool for me to just disrupt what you got going on. But Tati I don't want you going back to him," he explained with a calm desperation.

"Where was he this whole time?" I questioned. I didn't want to know at first, but I was curious. I loved Brevin, despite the way he treated me and to know he hadn't come to see me once while I was in the hospital told me more than a little bit. I was hoping he had good reasoning, but I couldn't think of one that would justify the way he'd vanished.

"Huh?"

"Tre'Wayne." I used his odd but sexy government name. It was hood and for some reason I liked that.

"He umm, Merce found him laid up with some bird."

"Oh."

I quickly wiped the tear that seeped from my eye because I didn't want it to hit Teflon's muscular chest that I was still lying on. However, the tears kept coming so I eventually had to lean my head back to wipe them. He noticed and caressed the side of my face while looking down at me. He pressed his lips against mine as I silently cried and even though I was hurt by Brevin's actions, having Teflon console me felt right… too right.

"Shhh, chill Tatiana. He ain't worth that shit." He thumbed some more of my tears and kissed me deeper and more gently.

He hugged me tightly, allowing his big strong frame to swallow mine and I just closed my eyes to enjoy it. My hands rubbed up and down the back of his head, even through his short kinky hair that was so soft. He placed kisses on my neck, before pulling back to crush his lips against mine. And just like that, we were at it again, making love like two long lost lovers.

***

I woke up around 8:30am, wrapped in Teflon's arms. My phone was going crazy, so I quickly snatched it from the nightstand. Squinting my eyes, I tapped the text message app to see who was blowing me up.

Jadynn: Mellow party went great. Now that you're out do you think you can work with me on the next one? It's an NBA player bachelor party at the same club.

Me: Yes! Please, I need to work!

Jadynn: K. I will let Eddie know, I love you.

Me: I love you too.

I hadn't worked in almost a fucking month, so I was ecstatic that my boss didn't fire me and that I could jump right back in. After texting Jadynn, I went to the conversation with my fiancé and me.

Brev: I wanna talk.

Brev: Tatiana. Are you feeling better?

Brev: *Where are you?*

Brev: *????*

I looked over my shoulder at a sleeping Teflon and gently peeled his sexy tatted arms from around my body. I really didn't want to because it was cold in the room, so being under the covers and cuddled up with him was currently life.

I grabbed my t-shirt and pulled it over my head, before tying my hair up and taking my toiletries to the bathroom. Sitting down on the toilet to pee, I finally decided to reply to Brevin.

Me: *Maybe another day.*

Brev: *Baby I am SORRY. I was tripping and shit, but I need to talk to you.*

I stared down at his text, contemplating. Why did I love him so? And most importantly how was I able to love him, while wanting to be with Teflon at the same time? Teflon was my fantasy and Brevin was my reality.

In a perfect world, I would run off with Teflon and fall in love, but I knew Brevin was where I belonged. He was normal. He was what I was used to. I refused to believe God would make me waste so much of my time on a man I wasn't supposed to be with. Then again, my feelings for Teflon were so fucking strong. Strong enough for me to sleep with him and I'd never thought about letting another man in my bed. I was so confused.

Suddenly I became disgusted with myself. I'd just miscarried almost a month ago and I'd had sex with another man. I ran my fingers through my hair, feeling my skin crawl in shame. Flashbacks of me delivering my baby who was dead already gave me a headache. I was supposed to be mourning, not sleeping around. My phone chiming ripped me from my thoughts.

Brev: Baby, I haven't seen you in almost a month.

Me: You didn't call. You didn't come see me. Where have you been? You knew where I was.

Brev: I was dealing with some shit.

Me: Right and I was just at a day spa.

Brev: Tati, please baby. I miss you. Don't you miss me? Come home and let's talk about this shit.

Me: Fine. I'll be there in an hour and a half.

I placed my phone on the counter and then proceeded to brush my teeth. Afterwards I tied my hair up into a bun and then removed the t-shirt. My body was damn near back to normal, but I still had a pudge towards the bottom. Because I was so small, no one would even notice unless you touched me.

I felt tears welling up as I examined my body. How many times was I going to be pregnant and never have a kid? I was tired of putting my body through all of these changes for nothing.

Shaking my head at myself and my life, I turned the shower on. Grabbing my soaps, I stepped inside and let the hot water run all over my body. My eyes were closed and I was silently praying that maybe Brevin and I could work things out, get married, and actually bring a kid to life.

I jumped at the sound of the shower curtain being tugged lightly.

Teflon was already inside with me, looking scrumptious as hell. Why was he so fine? His brown skin, ripped ass body, tattoos, kinky hair, and slanted eyes that he inherited from his Vietnamese mother, all contributed to his beyond handsome appearance.

"Did I scare you? You didn't hear me brushing my teeth?" he smiled widely, giving me full view of his perfect teeth. I just shook my head 'no', covering what little breasts I had as if he'd never seen me this way. "Don't cover up. I love everything about you." He gently unfolded my arms and pulled me into him to kiss on my neck.

"Teflon, you have to get out," I said lowly, eyes closed at the feeling of his lips on my neck.

He ignored me and lifted me up to bring me down onto his dick. This was so wrong, considering my situation, but I didn't want it to stop. Draping my arms around his neck, I moved my face closer to his to kiss him sensually. He glided me up and down on his dick with ease, proving I weighed nothing to a nigga like him. His slow steady strokes soon became rougher, making me cum almost immediately.

"Tef," I whimpered into his mouth as we tongued one another down.

"Tati, shit," he groaned, pounding into me under the shower water.

"Ahhh, uuuh!" I shrieked almost. He delivered a few more hard thrusts, before cumming inside of my body. We stood there kissing for a bit and then he finally let me down so we could clean up.

"Wanna go have breakfast?" he asked as we got dressed in the room.

"I can't, I'm going… I'm going home." I avoided eye contact. His brows dipped when his sexy face balled up.

"To Brevin."

"He umm, he wants to talk to me. And that's the least I could do—"

"The least you could do? He caused you to lose a baby that you'd carried for six months, his baby might I add, and he didn't come see you once Tatiana! You were in there recovering for almost a month! I- you know what, I don't give a fuck." He threw his hands up and then sat down to put his sneakers on.

"He is my fiancé, not you."

"Well next time you deliver a stillborn baby, make sure your fiancé is in the room with you and not a nigga who don't mean shit to you."

My heart dropped but there was nothing I could say. Teflon had done everything that Brevin should have, but I couldn't just jump ship.

There was an awkward silence as we continued to get ready. He was finished first, so he walked briskly by me, grabbing his car keys and wallet. His cologne danced up into my nostrils and lately it'd become a scent I looked forward to smelling.

"Tre'Wayne—" before I could finish the hotel door was slamming behind him.

I took an Uber to Walgreens so I could get a Plan B, but I wanted to make sure it was okay to take it considering what my body had just went through.

I exhaled sharply at my thoughts, as the Uber driver took me to Brevin's and my home in Ohio City. What the fuck was I thinking sleeping with Teflon like he was my husband?

"Thanks," I said once the driver pulled onto Jay Avenue. I took a deep breath and then pulled myself and my bag out of the car to go inside.

CHAPTER SIX

Brevin

I sat at the kitchen table with my leg bouncing, wondering where the fuck Tatiana was. Her little ass said she would be here in an hour and a half and it'd been two hours now. It was only thirty minutes, but so what? My time was precious. I had major shit to take care of, mainly getting my operation back on track since I ducked off for almost a damn month. Initially I only planned to chill with Amanda overnight to get my mind right, but when Groove told me Tatiana miscarried I didn't want to leave. I knew that shit was my fault, but it was mostly hers for being gone all fucking day like some hoe.

As I sat there downing a big ass bottle of water to clean my system out from drinking heavily last night, I heard someone stick their keys in the door. I turned to face it and waited as Tatiana walked in looking perfect. She had a glow to her and she didn't look upset at all, which kind of pissed me off. She should have been sad as hell right now.

"Hey," she mumbled, setting a duffle bag down which alarmed me.

"Why'd you have a duffle bag?"

"Jadynn brought it to me while I was in the hospital. I stayed with her and needed some clothes and things, Brevin." She sat down on the couch, sighing.

"So you were with her the whole time?"

"Uh no, I just got out of the hospital yesterday. Look what did you want to talk about?"

"Well firstly," I sat down next to her. "I want to apologize for contributing to the fact that you lost the baby and then disappearing for a little bit."

"Contributing? You were the sole reason." Her brows furrowed. I hated that she always played the fucking victim.

"Where were you that whole fucking day, Tati? I called you like six times and text you the same, but got nothing."

"I was with Jadynn, I told you. We had some things to do for the party that I never even got to work."

"And you were so busy you couldn't answer?" I glared at her. Tatiana would never step out on me because she knew better. And the only direction she could go would be down because no nigga was better than me.

"My phone was at the bottom of my purse, I got busy… so yes."

"Tati baby," I scooted closer to her and her body tensed up a bit as if she was afraid of me. "I'm sorry about the baby and I'm sorry about going missing for so long. I guess seeing your face would have been too hard for me."

"You have to grow up Brevin; you can't keep doing shit like this!

And you need to keep your fucking hands to yourself! I can't do this with you anymore. This is the second child that we've lost!" She shot up off the couch, tears streaming her golden cheeks.

"I get it! I'm just as sad Tatiana!" I looked up into her face. "I'm gonna get my shit together. Give me one more chance and I swear to you, you won't regret it."

She didn't say shit so I stood up to hold her close and kiss her lips. Our soft pecks soon became passionate tongue kisses, but when I tried to push her tights down she stopped me.

"Doctors said I can't yet."

"After a damn month?"

"Brevin."

"Okay, shit. Aight. My bad."

"I'm gonna go take a nap." She patted my chest and walked her little ass towards the stairs so she could go to the bedroom.

I wanted to stop her because something felt different. I didn't feel like we'd gotten everything squared away and that had me feeling slightly queasy. Usually every time I talked to Tatiana, she would respond much better and allow me to get some. This whole 'she still couldn't have sex' shit just didn't sit right with me, so I knew she was still angry.

I exhaled sharply as I watched her walk up the stairs. I wanted to follow her and demand that we make love, but my phone was jumping in my pocket and I knew whom it was. I'd finally left the bitch's crib two days ago and she'd been blowing me up ever since.

Amanda: We have to talk.

Brevin: I will be over there tomorrow or something.

Amanda: No, today Brevin.

Brevin: You don't run shit Amanda, I will be to you when I get good and fucking ready.

I stayed having to remind these bitches who the fucking boss was.

I shoved my phone back into my pocket after texting Groove. I needed to meet up with him and see what the fuck we were gonna do about getting me some damn security. That Teflon nigga was not an option, but I would be willing to allow that nigga Merce on. He seemed to have his head on straight unlike his homeboy, so if he was willing to get this money then I was cool with it. But, I still needed a second man and I wanted Groove to find him.

***

Later that night...

"Man, you need to have your ass at home with Tati," Groove sucked his teeth. We'd met up and talked at a lounge club and like always I ended up getting twisted.

"I am."

"I ain't coming back to get you tonight, nigga," he hissed, making me suck my teeth. I would have went home to Tatiana, but I was horny and Amanda said she needed to talk, so why not knock two birds out with one stone?

"Looks like I will be sleeping here then. Come back through around 10am. If you do it'll be something extra in your pay." I looked to him and he nodded.

"We need to feed the streets soon, Brevin. It's been a month since we've moved anything and niggas are talking about working with some other nigga all the way from Columbus."

"Tomorrow. Tomorrow shit will get straight. Just be here by 10am so I can get home to shower and all that shit."

"Aight." He nodded.

I shot Amanda a text and then climbed out making sure my piece was secured in my waist. Before I even finished coming up her steps, she was opening her front door, slightly scowling. I shook my head because I wasn't in the mood to deal with this shit right now. I needed to find me a mute bitch so I could fuck without having to hear her mouth.

"What's good?" I hugged her lightly and then slipped in past her.

"You're drunk."

"And?"

"I told you I needed to talk and you come over here late as hell, drunk off your ass? You think that's okay?" she folded her arms.

Amanda was cute and that was it. She was skinny with big boobs and no ass, but the pussy and mouth was fire, and her face was aight. She had nothing on Tatiana, but I started fucking her a lot more when I was staying up in her crib, as you know. I guess this past month made her think she had privileges that she really didn't have. I tell you, you give these hoes an inch and they'll take a fucking mile.

"Man, in a minute I'm gonna be out." I plopped down on the

couch, rubbing my hands down my face. I was drunk than a muthafucka. "What the fuck did you wanna talk about?"

"I'm pregnant, Brevin."

My face shot up out of my hands so quickly that I'd gotten a fucking crook in my neck.

"Pregnant? How? Nah you fucking lying!"

"What do you mean *how*? We've been fucking every night for the past month that's how!"

"Here," I stood up and peeled some cash off for her. "Get rid of that shit. I wanna see the paperwork to prove it as well."

"Brevin—"

My hand wrapping around her neck cut her sentence short real quick.

"Get rid of the shit ASAP. I don't want a fucking baby with you, especially after my fiancée just lost ours."

"This is ours too Brev—"

"I said get rid of it!" I banged her hand up against the wall.

I dropped her and she panted heavily while rubbing her neck all dramatically. If she didn't get that abortion willingly, I would have someone snatch the shit out of her then. No bitch was about to be having my kid if she wasn't Tatiana Drew.

CHAPTER SIX

Merce

The next morning...

$\mathcal{I}$ was sitting in my car outside of my parent's house on one. I'd just explained to them how Sebastian got locked up back in Los Angeles before I left and they were livid. Not at the fact that he was fucking up and got himself in jail, but at me for leaving him. I tried to explain that I only left for work in order to pay to get his ass a good lawyer. I mean yeah I still had funds left over from working for Luis, but shit I *did* have to take care of myself too. I couldn't just blow it all on this nigga's legal fees, especially when it was no longer revolving.

Sebastian was my brother but he was not my fucking child. I refused to neglect what the fuck I needed in life all because he couldn't get right.

I'd planned to tell my parents about his arrest as soon as I got here, but I knew that would be their reaction so I held off. Shit I didn't want to say anything this soon, but they kept asking me to tell him to come over, thinking he'd came back to Cleveland with me.

Shaking my head, I pulled from the curb and turned my music up. It was interrupted by a phone call, but when I saw it was Savannah I hit ignore. I wasn't in the mood to talk with her judgmental ass at all. At times I would try to see if we could work something out, because contrary to popular belief I didn't like the player life, but at the end of the day, Savannah just wasn't someone that I could see myself being with. I was looking for a girl who saw me as her man, not some little hood that she needed to guide and mold into what she wanted.

I made it to my favorite bar and threw my car into park. It was around 7pm on a Tuesday night, so it wasn't gonna be too crowded at all. I loathed being around a lot of people. Call me antisocial, but I hated having to converse with a lot of muthafuckas. Teflon was the same and that was something we bonded over. If it wasn't a bunch of sexy females, then we preferred to be on the quiet chill tip.

When I walked in I went straight to the bar, but out the corner of my eye, I spotted Jadynn. I hadn't seen her in a little over a month, but she looked sadder than the last time. Making my way over after ordering my drink, I stopped at her table. She didn't even see me, she just kept her eyes on the tabletop as she sipped some dark drink, slouching.

"Can I sit?" I questioned, snapping her from her trance.

She tousled her brownish red hair from one side to the other and sat up straight.

"Umm, sure. Merce right?" her brows dipped. I noticed that she didn't appear to have on any makeup, but she was beautiful without it;

most women were.

"Yeah, Jadynn right?" I smiled and slid my drink that the bartender delivered closer to me. "Did your dog die or something?"

"Why did you ask that?"

"You're sitting here all glum and shit, in a zone. I stood here at the table for like an hour, and you didn't even notice."

"It wasn't that long." She smiled shyly, pushing her long hair behind her ears.

"So you gon' tell me why you've been sad for a damn month or what? I hate seeing you like this and I don't even know you."

"I'm just going through something right now. I'm hoping it will pass soon." She fixed her leather jacket to cover up her small frame. "Why are you always here? Don't tell me you have a drinking problem."

"Nope. I'm just going through something like you."

"Like what?"

"So you want me to tell you my business, while you keep yours a secret? It don't work like that baby but nice try." I nodded my head up to the bartender so I could get a refill.

She chuckled lowly, making one dimple appear in her cheek. She was beautiful, but in that natural way. She had that classic beauty, the shit we didn't see anymore these days. Every girl had her ass plumped up and her titties filled with some fake shit. And if they did have real assets, they kept them on display like a hoe. But Jadynn, she was just a regular girl, I liked that. Well at least she seemed like just a regular girl.

"You were right," she sighed.

"About what?"

"About me having a problem with a man, he wasn't worth shit. You were right about that part too."

"Is that what you're still upset over?" I turned my lip up.

I hoped she wasn't one of them females who let niggas dog them and made excuses on reasons to stay. No offense to Tatiana, but that shit was weak as hell. The only pass Tatiana got was that she was pregnant by the nigga, and I knew it was hard for women to abandon a nigga that they were pregnant by.

"Not him necessarily, but some events involving him." Her voice trailed off at the end, as she let her pointing finger travel around the rim of the cup.

"Well don't let that shit fuck with you. You're too young and pretty for that shit. And you don't have kids with him right?"

"No."

"Then move on." I shrugged, tossing my drink back.

"So where is your woman? I know you have one floating around Cleveland by now. Oh wait, you're from here, so there are some old ones for sure."

I laughed because she was right.

"I don't have a woman per say. I have friends though, chicks I'm cool with."

"Cool meaning they let you fuck?"

"Cool meaning we chill, talk through text, and sometimes yeah we fuck. I wouldn't call any of them my woman though."

"Let me guess, you're not the relationship type."

"No, that's not true, I just refuse to settle. And it's not like I'm itching to be in a relationship, so I wouldn't say that I'm looking either. If I meet someone then great, but if not…" I shrugged. She nodded in response before polishing off what was in her cup.

"Well I think I'm gonna only have friends for a while."

"Can I be one of them?" I cocked my head slightly, admiring every detail of her face. Her dimples were deep, appearing every time she pursed her full lips.

"I don't know. I'm not looking for that type of friend." She cheesed.

"I'm the best type of friend to have, because I can be any type you want. I'm a good listener, I tell pretty good jokes if you're feeling frisky one night I can help with that too." I threw my hand up to tell the bartender to get me another.

"Shit, why not." She shrugged.

We sat there talking for a little longer before deciding to leave. She rode in an Uber here like a smart person, but since I was good enough to drive she hopped into my whip. I drove her to my new spot, even though I didn't have much furniture yet. I could tell she wasn't the type to judge off of that shit, unlike Savannah. Her ass would be reprimanding me the whole time, telling me how to fix my place up.

"This place is nice." Jadynn smiled as we entered my spot.

"I don't have much shit, but I have a couch, an air mattress, a lamp, and a fridge." I chuckled lightly as I hit the lights.

She walked in, tousling her hair as she scanned the place with her eyes. I locked the door behind her and then moved my computer off the couch so she could sit down.

"You must have just moved here. Tatiana told me you guys were living with Brevin." She sat down, removing her leather jacket. She had this top on that showed her flat stomach.

"Yeah it was just a temporary thing though. Are you hungry? I can make you a snack out of what I got."

"I can't see you making a snack. You don't have that look."

"What types of niggas make snacks?" I smiled since she was laughing so hard. She literally lit up the room with her laugh.

"I don't know. You're too rough around the edges. You seem like you can only make burgers and steaks on a grill, if that."

"Well I can make you a bomb ass parfait." As soon as the words left my mouth, she fell over, cracking up and clapping her hands.

"I'm sorry. I'm so sorry, that's just hilarious. But yes, I would love a parfait."

"Aight baby. Laugh all you want but this shit is about to change your world."

She just continued to chuckle as I walked around the bar into my kitchen to wash my hands. I grabbed the granola, yogurt, and fruit from the fridge, and began strategically stacking it into some small mason jars I'd gotten. I learned all this shit from when I was flat broke. You become creative when you don't have money. But even now that I was much better off, I still enjoyed shit like this.

"Here you go." I handed her one of the small mason jars with a spoon in it.

"Thanks, Merce. What's in it?"

"Granola, blueberries, blackberries, strawberries, and vanilla yogurt."

"Here goes." She smiled and shoved a spoonful into her mouth. I hadn't seen her smile this much in my life, but then again I'd only seen her ass about three times. "Oh my gosh! This is actually good. Where did you learn this?"

"I just threw some shit together one night out of what I had."

"Hard times?" Her facial expression softened as she continued to eat. She was tearing the shit up, boosting my ego a little bit.

"Yeah, but I'm good now. I mean a nigga ain't rich or nothing, but I can shop, pay bills, and take a nice girl out to eat." I ate some of the parfait, looking at her out the corner of my eye.

"Are you asking me on a date?"

"No, I was just trying to get you to understand my financial situation."

"Oh because if you were asking me, on a friendly outing, I would have said yes. But since you weren't, I don't know what to say."

I chuckled at her, shaking my head.

"I for real wasn't asking you out, but I already told you I wanted to be your friend and shit. So fuck it, let's do something one of these days."

"Okay. I don't have set off days, but once I know what day I'm free I will text you. Wait, I need your number."

I pulled my iPhone from my pocket and passed it to her so she could type hers in. I called her and once my number popped up I hung up.

"A Cleveland number? You've been in Los Angeles this whole time though." She frowned.

"I know. Tef and I changed our shit a few weeks after we moved. We didn't want anybody from California calling us. Nothing's back there that we need. Only person who has my number is my little brother."

"Yeah? He didn't come back with you?"

"Nah, he umm, he got into some shit. But he'll be back soon, if he wants to come."

"Do you plan to ever go back?"

"Nah." I shook my head.

"Good." She half smiled.

We talked all night until we got tired, and once we were, we removed our jackets and shoes, before lying on the air mattress together. We didn't cuddle or anything, but we weren't awkwardly distant either while on the bed. We just talked, as we listened to soft music on Pandora until we fell asleep.

I was looking forward to making her pretty ass a very good friend of mine.

CHAPTER SIX

Teflon

One week later…

$\mathcal{I}$ was chilling in my new spot, smoking a blunt. I'd been on some bullshit lately because I couldn't get Tatiana off my fucking mind for shit. I was already into her little ass, but after we had sex, shit got intense for me. I wasn't even the type of nigga to gain feelings for a woman just because I had sex with her, but I guess God was giving me a taste of my own medicine.

All my life I've always had the upper hand, but with Tatiana I was at her mercy. I could barely get my dick wet with other bitches because the pussy just wasn't the same as hers. I'd only had the shit three times and I was already hooked on it like a fucking junkie. I'd never had pussy that good in my life, not even from Kayla. I wasn't sure if it was all the emotions and feelings traveling back and forth between us as we made love or what, but I was straight bugging. Her little ass had me in the palm of her hand and I didn't like that shit at all. Not one damn bit.

Irritated by my thoughts, I ashed the blunt and stared into the mirror leaning up against the wall. My place was pretty much in tact since Merce and I paid top dollar to have our shit moved in and put in place. I would never do that shit again, because two of my fucking bookshelves got scratched up. If the shit was old that would be one thing, but everything in here was brand spanking new and I didn't appreciate them muthafuckas scraping it. I had to talk myself out of popping them niggas a few times.

"Shit," I grumbled as I stood to my feet.

I made my way to the bathroom and cut the shower on. After taking a piss, I washed my hands and then brushed my teeth while the water warmed up. Once I was done flossing and rinsing, I hopped into the shower and washed thoroughly. Getting out, I wrapped a towel around my waist and went to get my iPhone from the kitchen. I pulled up Merce's name and shot him a text.

Me: Strip club?

Merce: Nah, watching a movie.

Me: Nigga you'd rather watch a movie than see some pussy?

Merce: Kind of, I gotta little something over here.

Me: Savannah's bougie ass.

Merce: Nah, Tatiana's friend Jadynn.

Me: Oh, fasho. Enjoy.

I shook my head with a smile at my boy. I was low-key jealous that he was able to chill with Jadynn, since Tatiana had played me to the left. She straight put that fire ass pussy on me and dropped me, just like I be doing these hoes. I guess I deserved it.

I text my cousin Groove to see if he was down and since he was I went ahead and got dressed.

Tonight I was gonna make sure I forgot about Tatiana. I was done with that bullshit. I was a thug and thugs didn't sit around crying over some pussy they didn't even know like that. No matter how good it was and no matter how dope the chick was.

***

"Aye, I wanna talk to you." Groove sipped his beer as we watched this thick white bitch dance on stage. She reminded me a lot of Ice-T's wife Coco.

"About?"

"A job."

"Shit I'm all ears. I definitely need some work, you know that."

"Come back to work for Brevin man. Wait… let me talk. I know you don't fuck with him because of what he did to his girl, but you have to remember that's his girl, Teflon. You wouldn't want some nigga trying to tell you how to treat Kayla, right?"

"Man, I fucked around on Kayla I didn't beat her."

"I mean Brevin don't even be hitting her like that, he just gets rough with her sometimes and if he's drunk he may do extra."

"Extra? You call beating her until she lost her damn baby, extra?" I frowned and looked over at him. I was about ready to whoop this nigga's ass right now.

"Tef, I get it. He was foul for that, but my point is that Tatiana is his woman, not yours, not mine, and not Merce's. Just get paid and look the other way."

"I can't just look the other fuckin' way and you shouldn't either."

He was quiet, so I glanced over at him to see he was wearing a confused expression.

"Tef, please tell me you didn't fuck his girl."

"I don't know what you're talking about, my nigga." I shook my head repeatedly as I gulped some of my beer down.

"I ain't never known you to give a fuck about what another nigga was doing with his bitch, but now you're willing to give up a fat paycheck for Tati?"

"It's not for her, it's the principle."

"Did you fuck her, Tre'Wayne?"

I knew he was serious because he used my first name. I didn't want to tell him, because I didn't want to talk about it. I wasn't worried that he would tell Brevin, because Groove was my cousin at the end of the day and he knew better. But out of respect I didn't want to put Tatiana out there like that.

"I haven't touched her; I just don't like what he did. If he was just cheating that's one thing, but I can't stand around and watch a nigga pulverize a woman that's a quarter his size. The girl is fucking 5'1, one hundred pounds soaking wet! He has no business putting his hands on her!"

"I agree, totally! But just get the money. And Tef I know you, so if you haven't fucked her you plan on fucking, or you want to at the least."

"Nope."

"Well just think about getting back on. He's open to the idea and remember he's paying $30,000 *minimum.*"

"Mhm."

I wasn't paying this nigga any mind. I wasn't working for Brevin and that was the fucking end of the shit.

We chilled in the club for a couple more hours and finally, I was leaving, but not without a companion. This bitch named Rebecca, who was stacked like a muthafucka, couldn't wait to get in my bed, and I couldn't wait to bend her ass over and go to town.

We made it to my place about fifteen minutes later, arriving at around 11pm. I was low-key hella twisted, so I was happy I didn't drive. Uber was a lifesaver right now.

"Make yourself comfortable," I told her as I led her to the living room.

"This place is beautiful," she giggled. I gave her a fake one back, because Tatiana was still on my mind.

I was gonna pour us some drinks, but I was drunk enough already wanted to get to fucking. I planned to never see her ass again so no need to make conversation.

I walked up to Rebecca as she sat on my couch smiling and began to caress her hair. She immediately caught on, because she began unbuckling my jeans. Reaching into my boxers, she released my dick while I took my shirt off.

"Damn," I grumbled as she began sucking me up.

I let my head fall back as she went to work on me, letting her spit flow freely. I massaged her hair, but quickly stopped when I felt something hard under it. I'm guessing this shit was a weave, but I wasn't sure.

As I was getting close to busting my nut, someone started beating on my door. I tried to ignore it and continued humping her face, but the person was relentless with their knocking.

"Fuck!" I hollered, sliding my dick out of Rebecca's mouth.

I stuffed myself back into my pants and darted towards my door to look through the peephole. The person standing there caused my jaw to drop and my heart rate to speed up. Tatiana.

I cleared my throat and looked around as if I would be able to find something on the floor to help me with this situation. She knocked again and I was surprised that such a small girl had so much strength. I finally took a deep breath and opened the door just enough to let my face peek out.

"Tati, it's almost midnight."

"I need to talk to you," she sniffled, wiping tears from her eyes. I couldn't turn her away, but damn if this wasn't the wrong time.

"Okay—"

"Teflon!" Rebecca called out, making me close my eyes in irritation.

"Move." Tatiana barged in past me walking fast as fuck like she was really about to do some shit with her little ass.

"Rebecca—"

"Go! Get the fuck out, bitch," Tatiana cut in.

"I didn't know you had a girlfriend, Teflon—"

"Well now you know bitch, so go!"

"You ain't gonna keep calling me a bitch!"

"Bitch." Tatiana got her little ass in Rebecca's face, so I picked her up from behind and held her in my arms.

"Rebecca, go. Please."

Rebecca stared at Tatiana, as I held her in my arms. She shouted obscenities and threats as Rebecca made her way out. She reminded me of those Shih Tzu poodles that never stopped barking and didn't care how big the other dog was.

Once Rebecca was out the door, I placed Tatiana to her feet. She shoved the shit out of me and I stumbled back even though her ass was no bigger than a minute. I just walked away to lock up.

"What the fuck is all this for?" I barked, coming back from locking my door.

"Why did you have her here?"

"Are you serious right now?" I chuckled angrily, because I couldn't believe she was mad about another bitch being in my crib, while she had a fiancé she wouldn't leave.

"Yes I'm serious! So you just sleep with every girl you run into?"

"No, I don't. Tatiana, baby why are you mad? You have Brevin, yet you're here at my crib causing a ruckus at nearly midnight."

"You haven't even called me!"

"I don't have your damn number!"

She paused for a moment, staring at me before we both chuckled together. She finally plopped down onto the couch and stared down at her hands while fidgeting. I made my way over to her and kneeled down so that I could look up into her perfect face. When I moved her short brown hair behind her shoulder, I saw a deep bruise on her collarbone.

"Is this why you're here?" I brushed my thumb against it and she swiftly moved away.

"That's old."

"How old?"

"A week."

"And you're still with that nigga." I stood to my feet and paced the floor. I was mad all over again. She came over here with this bullshit, kicking muthafuckas out of my spot and for what? So she could use me for the night and go back to her nigga? Fuck that shit. "Look Tati, you gotta go. I'm sleepy."

She picked her face up and my chest started to tighten. Despite the few tears that traveled down her face, she was still beautiful. I wanted to yank her ass off my couch and throw her out of my spot but I couldn't.

"Let me just stay here with you tonight," she sniffled, standing up. She was so small, that it was almost comical because I was much taller and more muscular.

"And then what happens in the morning?" I didn't like the way she had me feeling. My mind and train of thought was all fucked up over her. She shrugged as a response, making me scoff. "Tell me. What will happen in the morning? You're gonna wake up and run back to his ass? Tell me!" I hollered down into her face even though I didn't mean to.

"I can't just do what you want me to do! I don't even know you and you want me to leave my fiancé for you!"

"At this point Tatiana, I don't give a fuck who you leave the nigga for, as long as you leave! And if you're gonna stay and let him continue to fuck you up, then please don't seek me again."

I Got Your Back ◆ *Teflon & Tatiana's Love Story*

CHAPTER SIX

Tatiana

$\mathcal{I}$ stared up into Teflon's face as he panted angrily. I understood where he was coming from one hundred percent, but it was more complicated than that. It wasn't as easy as it sounded and honestly I didn't know Teflon. Yeah he was a nice guy, handsome as ever and all that jazz, but so was Brevin when he wanted to be. And to make matters worse, Brevin was the king of Cleveland. Teflon and I would only last for a hot second before something happened to us. There was a lot to think about and I wanted him to understand that.

"Tef, leaving Brevin is more than *leaving* him." I sat back down and he followed suit.

"What?" he scowled, looking sexy as hell.

I tied my short curly hair up into a bun and then removed my jacket since I was a little hot.

"Leaving Brevin means that he may kill me, us and whomever we're affiliated with. You have to remember that he would never just let me go that easily."

"Ain't nobody scared of him."

"I know. I know you're not. But a lot of people are and they will do whatever he wants them to do, including harm me. Is that what you want?"

"What I want is for you to let him go. I'm not saying to be with me, because frankly I don't know if I'm ready for all of that yet. I just don't want him to do anything to you that could be fatal, Tati."

Him saying that he wasn't ready to be in a relationship with me felt like a punch to the stomach. I knew I wasn't ready to just move from a fiancé to another man, but I guess I assumed he wanted me more seriously. His statement just proved why I couldn't make any rash decisions right now, like leaving Brevin and shacking up with him as *friends*.

"There has to be a plan in place, Tef."

"What?" he furrowed his brows again.

"You have to have a plan, or help me devise one so that I can leave."

"The only way he'll let you go with no problems is if he's in the damn ground and I know you don't want that." I didn't say anything so he looked to me and asked, "Do you want that?"

"I wouldn't ask you to do something like that."

"You don't have to."

I just nodded.

"So can I stay here for the night please?"

"Yeah."

We both stood up, but before I could move, he was kissing me and taking my hair down. He tongued me down with so much passion, that I couldn't do anything but stand there and reciprocate. We undressed one another slowly, before he scooped me up and carried me to the bedroom. Placing me on the bed, he walked off and went into the bathroom to do something. I heard water running and stuff moving, before he finally emerged.

"You okay?" I asked still lying under the covers naked.

"I just had to wash old girl off of me."

"You fucked her?"

"I got a little bit of head, nothing more."

I stayed quiet as he climbed under the covers and got in between my legs. We made eye contact as he placed my legs in the nook of his arms, before kissing my lips gently. I felt some type of way about having sex with him when there was no commitment and technically, I was still with Brevin, but I wanted this. I loved the way he made me feel, not just in bed but overall. It was way better than Brevin had ever made me feel.

"I lied Tati," he groaned as he plunged into me while sucking my neck. That was too much pleasure at once.

I was moaning so I couldn't really respond to him. I hadn't slept with Brevin since before I miscarried, so Teflon was the last person I'd had sex with.

When I was finally about to say something, his lips crushed against mine, while his big hands groped me everywhere possible.

"I want you to be mine baby," he grumbled.

"Tef," I moaned, letting my hands rub up and down his strong back.

He continued to slide in and out of me with precision, while kissing me passionately. I didn't know what to say to him or how to answer. It wasn't that I didn't want him, because believe me I did from the moment I first saw him. It was just that I was unsure. All that I was sure about right now was that I wanted out with Brevin and to be able to live my life freely once he and I were over.

Teflon lifted himself up, placed one hand on his headboard while the other gripped my thigh. We moaned loudly together as he rammed into me, sweat dripping from his sexy face and body. We were both drenched, but too into the moment to stop and cut the air on.

"Ahh, uuuh, aaah!" I called out as he continued to pummel my center. I knew I was gonna be sore in the morning.

"Mmm, fuck." He tucked his lips in, slowing down his pumps. Finally, he slid out and helped me up. "These are so small," he chuckled before taking my nipple into his mouth. "I love them though," he said before forcing his tongue down my throat.

Once he pulled away, he placed me on all fours, and pushed into me. Taking my hair into his hands, he thrust into me nice and slowly, making me cry out every single time. I shivered from releasing, which only made him moan. After hitting my spot slow motion style, he picked up his pace, beating it up until we both came. I stayed in the same position as he kissed all over my back, sucking certain places that made me quiver.

"Tef, you forgot to pull out," I whined.

"I'm sorry," he mumbled, continuing to kiss all over me.

We had no business fucking raw when we didn't even know each other, but for some reason every time we did it, we went without.

We finally caught our breaths, so we got out of the bed to go shower together. It ended up turning into another round before we for real washed off and returned to the bed.

"Are my breasts really that small?" I questioned as I laid on his chest, circling his tattoos with my fingers. I already knew the answer because people used to make fun of me and say I had two backs in high school.

"I mean you're not flat chested, but they are the smallest I've ever seen. I like them though. I like everything about you, especially your legs. It's not much of them, but they're sexy as hell."

"Really?" I picked my head up and smiled at him. He nodded with a serious expression. Brevin always told me I was beautiful, when he wasn't insulting me, but he never pointed anything out specifically. Not that it mattered I guess… but then again I guess it did matter to me.

"Yeah really. I love when you show them. I love your body. Your butt and breasts may not be big and you may be short, but you definitely have a little meat on you. You're perfect." He looked deeply into my eyes as he always did.

"Thank you—"

He pressed his lips against mine and we sucked one another's for a few before finally pulling away.

"I'm serious about what I said baby, it's not just because I was inside you."

"About being with me?" My head was resting on his chest again.

"Yeah. And believe me I know it's crazy because we just met and shit. And not only are you in a relationship, but I just ended a serious one too. However… I just can't help how I feel. After our hotel stint, you had me on some other shit these past few weeks."

"What do you mean?"

"You had a nigga sitting in the corner nursing a bottle in the dark," he replied and we both chuckled.

"You may not believe me, but I was miserable too," I admitted.

The past couple weeks of being away from Teflon and not talking to him were killing me. I tried to make myself get over it by remembering that I didn't know him that well to be yearning for him, but it never worked. Every time I closed my eyes, I would think or dream about him. I would reminisce on our time together so hard that I would forget where I was going or what I was doing.

I'd never missed someone so much in my life. It was almost as if I'd become dependent on him in just that short amount of time. I felt unsafe without him living in the house anymore and angry at the thought of him entertaining another girl. I eventually became fed up over tossing and turning every night because I couldn't get him off of my mind. That's how I ended up over here at almost midnight.

"I'm happy to hear that shit low-key. I thought I was the only one bugging."

"No," I whispered. "I was going through it too. My chest ached every time you crossed my mind, because I thought I would never see or talk to you again."

"Damn, it's the same with me." He sucked his teeth. "Fuck does all that shit mean?"

"Have you ever felt that way about someone else?" I pressed my chin into his chest in order to stare into his eyes.

"Never. I've never felt like a certain woman could tell me to jump and I'd ask how high. But with you, it was almost like I was waiting by an imaginary phone for you. Hoping you would call me."

I watched his face twist into confusion as he explained his feelings. His hand had stopped rubbing up and down my back, signaling that he was in deep thought and couldn't do it and another thing at once. It was obvious that he'd truly never felt what he was currently feeling because he didn't understand it. I didn't understand what we had either. It couldn't be love because I didn't know him. Then again, it wasn't a simple crush or adoration, because the feelings we shared were too powerful.

"So what should we do?"

"I don't even know. I just know I want you in any way that you'll have me. From the first time I saw you, I just wanted to be close to you. I didn't know in what way yet, but I had to be near you."

My heart literally turned to mush when those words left his mouth. The fact that he was willing to take anything I gave him, anything that would keep him close to me caused goose bumps to arise on my arms.

"I know what you mean, that's why you caught me staring into your room." I giggled shyly.

"Yeah, I knew I had you."

"No you didn't!" I smacked his chest lightly as we laughed in unison.

"Nah, but I'm feeling like I need you or something." His tone was low, raspy, raw, and honest as he brushed his thumb across my cheek, while looking into my eyes. I let my arm rest across his chiseled abs, not losing eye contact with him once.

"Me too," I said in a low tone before our lips met and our tongues began to dance.

CHAPTER SEVEN

Teflon

The next morning…

I woke up pretty early this morning to shower, brush my teeth, and run to the grocery store really quickly. By the time I got back, I heard the shower running so I knew Tatiana was in there. I shook my head as I thought about last night, while taking out what I needed to make French toast.

The night before was intense as fuck, but I didn't feel like she was on her bullshit, which was a plus. I still didn't like the fact that she had such a hold on me, because if she did go back to that nigga yet again, I may be worse off. At least before, she didn't really know my thought process but after spilling my fucking guts, her going back would be like a fucking dagger to the chest.

If Kayla were here to witness this shit right now, she would be floored for sure, because I wasn't this type of nigga at all. A bitch was lucky if I even replied to her text after we fucked, so the fact that Tatiana had me ready to show up at Brevin's crib and demand to see her was some crazy shit. But my mama always told me I would meet a girl that would have me wrapped around her finger. I always thought that it would be Kayla, just down the line. I had no idea it would be some little shorty from Cleveland who stopped at my abs.

Speaking of the devil, as I buttered the pan I saw that Kayla was calling me. This wasn't really the best time to talk, so I was gonna let that shit go to voicemail. I didn't wanna give her my number when I changed it, but I felt like not giving it to her was foul.

The ringing ceased and my phone dinged to let me know I had a voicemail, then again to say it was a text.

I finished preparing the only breakfast dish I knew how to cook and right when I was placing the fruit on, Tatiana walked in wrapped in a towel.

Despite her lacking in certain areas physically, she was the sexiest woman I'd ever laid eyes on. I watched her sexy legs as she made her way over to me and licked my lips at the thought of them sitting on my shoulders while I sucked on her pussy.

"Good morning. I was looking for you." She walked right up to me and we kissed. Our bodies both reacted, so after we pulled away we went right back in for another.

"I didn't have what I needed to make you breakfast."

"Thank you." She chuckled, flashing her big beautiful smile. I kissed the side of her face as she picked the plate up.

We sat down at my bar to eat. At first, it was quiet as we dug in. Every time I cooked this shit, it got better.

"I don't have any clothes here." She broke the silence.

"I can take you to the mall and we can get whatever you need."

"Teflon, I have to go home at some point or Brevin will come looking for me."

I stabbed a couple pieces of French toast as I thought about what she was saying. I didn't want her around that nigga if I wasn't present, but I knew she was right. If she just disappeared the nigga would go crazy looking for her and right now, I wasn't prepared to protect her. I mean I could against Brevin himself, easily, I've done it before when I whooped his ass the night she lost her baby. But what I couldn't do was go against his team, by myself, or even if I had Merce with me. My main goal *wasn't* to make sure I was good, it was to make sure she was. This was all about her. She'd consumed me in such a short matter of time and I didn't know if that was good or bad.

"Aight, but you're not spending the night. Go, get some shit that will last you at least a couple weeks and then come back. I will buy you anything else.

"What will I say to him then?" Her face was knotted.

"Tell him it's a work trip. I'm sure he'll be happy to know you're gonna be traveling and shit for some time."

"What is that supposed to mean?"

"Nothing Tati. Eat your food and when you're done put your number in my phone. If anything happens before you get out, hit me."

"What did you mean by what you said, Teflon?"

I sighed before saying, "Tatiana you know he wasn't faithful to you. That's what I mean, if you must know." She just turned from me and continued eating her food. "I didn't mean to throw it in your face. It was a thought in my head that just came out." I kissed the corner of her mouth.

"Are you any different?" She looked to me.

"I wasn't, no."

"You mean with Kayla."

"Yeah, but you already know that I feel differently about you."

"How do you know this will be different, Teflon? What if you start acting like Brevin? Or how you acted while with Kayla?"

"Because I haven't thought about another woman or wanted to be with another woman since I met you, baby. And especially after we made love the first time."

"Then what was Rebecca?"

"Just something to help keep my mind off of you."

I pecked her lips a few times, before our kisses became hungrier and more passionate. I took her towel off and we got to it right on the floor.

Afterwards we cleaned ourselves up and she left to go get some clothes and shit, but not before putting her number in my phone and calling herself. Once she was gone, I cleaned up a little bit and almost like clockwork Kayla was calling me again. Since Tatiana wasn't here, I decided to go ahead and answer.

"Damn, are you that busy?" she spat as soon as I accepted the call.

"Kind of, you know I just got here a couple months ago, Kay. I'm still getting shit together, so there are gonna be times where I'm tied up." I was kind of irritated by her actions. She was on the same tip she was on when I was her man and I wasn't anymore.

"Whatever nigga, that's just code for you were with another bitch."

See.

"And what if I was, Kayla?"

"Then that would be shady as fuck and we would have a problem nigga! You went to Cleveland to get work remember? Not to get with other bitches, even if it's just to bust a nut!"

I couldn't help myself so I burst into laughter.

"Kayla man—"

"Did I say something funny, nigga? Let me find out that you're out in Ohio living the player life, Tre'Wayne!"

"Okay." I chuckled lightly because she didn't realize how stupid she sounded. I was gonna do what the fuck I wanted to regardless. If she couldn't control me when we were in the same state, what made her think she could while we were miles apart? But most importantly, I wasn't her fucking nigga.

"Okay what?" she pulled me from my thoughts.

"Just okay, I don't have a response to that. I really don't get why you're acting like this when you broke up with me."

"But you promised me that you would work on yourself, meaning that you weren't gonna be focused on whores. I got the impression that you were gonna find some discipline somewhere and then come back to me with some damn sense!"

"Okay," I sighed, rubbing my hand down my face.

"Stop saying that shit!" she hollered so loudly that it immediately changed my mood.

"Aye, calm yo' silly ass down, Kayla! Don't call me on this bullshit no muthafucking more! I'm not yo' nigga and you damn sure ain't my bitch so the next time you wanna call me trying to put me in my place you need to remember that you broke up with me!"

As soon as I was done yelling, I heard sniffling.

"So I can't change my mind?"

"Change your mind?"

"Yeah. I talked to my mom and she was telling me that I should work with you and that you probably just had a problem."

"I don't have a problem, Kayla. But look I gotta handle some shit. Talk to you later."

"Tef—"

I hung up the phone before she could even finish. I wasn't trying to hear shit she was saying. Not because I was off her, but because I didn't want to hear her tell me she wanted to be back together. Technically she did nothing wrong in our relationship, and I would feel fucked up if I told her I didn't want to be with her anymore. I knew she wouldn't understand how I could have moved on already and shit I didn't really get it either, so it would be difficult as hell to explain.

It was best that I just ignore her ass for right now, until I could get my thoughts together and actually let her know the real. I'd let her know the real in a way that she would at least be able to process. I didn't know how I would be able to do that, but one thing I did know was that I wanted Tatiana Drew and nobody else.

***

"Hey Ma, what are you cooking?" I walked into my mother's home located in Corlett. It was an okay neighborhood, but once I got my funds up I would be moving her out of here.

"Some soup, would you like some?" She smiled.

"Nah Ma, you need to cook for my black side," I joked, making her burst into laughter.

"You sound just like your father. I had no idea how to make heavy foods like that until we got together you know?"

"I know. But you make the best fried chicken now."

"The best?" She smiled.

"Nah, but I fuck with it. I mean I like it," I clenched my teeth together. I hadn't been around my mom this much in a long time, since I was living in another state, so I would have to get used to not cursing around her anymore.

"Want some green iced tea?"

"Okay." I nodded as I sat down on the couch. "Now you're speaking to my Asian side," I taunted and we laughed.

"How is Kayla?" she brought me the iced tea and sat down on the couch a little ways down from me.

"Ma, I told you the last time I came over here that she and I don't talk like that anymore."

"You need to try to get her back, Tre'Wayne. She loves you, even though you've done some bad things to her. You need to propose."

"Absolutely not." I shook my head 'no' as I drank the tea.

"Why?"

"Because I'm not ready to get married Ma. I can barely be a good boyfriend, let alone husband."

"You need to grow up, Tre'Wayne. You're gonna be thirty in just two short years and you're still living like you're twenty-one. I don't want you being like Torrey. Baby I'm happy you came back to Ohio, but you need to get Kayla back or move her out here."

I knew I shouldn't have let Kayla meet my mom.

"I'm never gonna be like Torrey and you know that."

"Look at Thomas, he's your little brother and he knows the value of a good woman when he sees one. He's in Paris studying, yet stills find time for Cameron," she boasted about my little brother and his little girlfriend. "Even Ryan does right by that Cecily girl," she spoke, referring to my cousin Groove and his baby mama.

"Ma, what if I met somebody else?" I set my glass on the coaster and looked over to see her perplexed expression. It was slightly comical.

"How? Where? Here in Cleveland?"

"Possibly."

"It's a yes or no question baby."

"Yeah I met a girl out here and that shi— mess is complicated as… heck. She has a fiancé, well she did, but she wants to be with me and I wanna be with her. We kind of have to keep it a secret though until further notice."

"Why would you subject yourself to such a stressful situation with some new girl when you could have a sweet, caring girl like Kayla?"

"Because I don't want Kayla Ma, I want her."

She paused for a moment and her face and body language softened.

"What's her name?"

"Tatiana," I sighed, scratching my head before pulling my hood back over it.

"Could you see yourself marrying her?"

"Yes and that's what I don't get. I've been with Kayla for years and I've always told myself I would marry her but I just couldn't bring myself to ask. When I thought about being her husband it made me cringe. Not because of her but because I didn't want to be tied to her like that, or any other woman. But with Tatiana, just thinking about putting a ring on her finger and her having my baby makes me feel some type of way, in a good way though. How is that shit possible?"

"It happens, Tre'Wayne. Love can happen in one week or in one year." I was happy she said nothing about me cursing. "But if Tatiana is so special then I must meet her."

"We'll see." I half smiled before looking off.

Tatiana had me all out of whack.

CHAPTER SEVEN

Tatiana

An hour earlier...

$\mathcal{I}$ slipped my key into the knob and entered the house slowly. I'd text Brevin earlier to let him know that I left early this morning to get a head start on work. He went to bed around 10pm last night, so he had no idea that I slipped out around 11:30pm. He thought I was gonna be working until late tonight. I only told him that because I didn't know how long I was gonna be with Teflon. Time seemed to fly by whenever I was with him. It would be midnight and then I would look up to see it was 6am. We would just be conversing or having sex as if it was nothing.

Just thinking about him brought a smile to my face, but the thought that he and I were just in a phase did bother me a bit. I wasn't one to develop false feelings so I wasn't worried about me, but men loved a chase and once the chase ended, so did their admiration. I didn't want to fall head over heels for a man who was living in the moment. However, at the end of the day I needed to leave Brevin no matter what.

I made my way up the stairs, silently praying that Brevin would go for this work trip thing. I planned to tell him that Jadynn and I were working a party out in Cincinnati, so we needed to spend the night in a hotel out there. If he was in a good mood he would go for it, but if not I may have a problem.

Nearing the bedroom door, I took a deep breath before slowly turning the knob. I slowly opened the door and the sight before me almost made me throw up. There Gloria was, getting fucked by *my* man in *my* bed, doggy style. This was wrong in so many ways, not only because Brevin and I were engaged, but because this was his best friend's girlfriend.

I was frozen as I watched them fuck like they'd done this millions of times. How long had this been going on? And did Mack know about it? The shit made me sick; especially with the way she would be smiling in my face and trying to bond with me like she wasn't one of the many hoes sucking my man's dick.

I was going to burst in there, cause a scene, and use that as reason to leave Brevin, but that would never work. He would hunt me down and profess his love constantly in hopes of me taking him back. I needed him to believe that I wasn't in town so that he wouldn't bother me.

The two lovebirds finally finished and Gloria laid back onto the bed, head pressed onto my fucking pillow.

"Aye, you gotta go." Brevin shook her lightly.

"What? You said Tatiana would be back late," she frowned,

running her fingers through her cheap ass weave.

"Yeah but I have shit to do and since I'm gonna be handling business I don't need you hanging around here. Plus Mack is coming through."

"He knows we fuck."

My eyes almost fell out of my head when she said that.

"He knows but that doesn't mean I like throwing the shit up in his face. Now hurry the fuck up while I shower."

She sucked her teeth and climbed out of the bed. I darted away and went into the bedroom down the hall, then waited until I heard Brevin's and my bedroom door close. When I peeked out, I saw Gloria heading down the stairs, so I went back into the room and waited about ten minutes. I then came out and entered my bedroom to see Brevin smoking a blunt, ass naked.

"Tati!" he almost jumped out of his skin as he scoured the room for something to cover himself with.

"Why are you naked?" I played dumb.

"I was about to shower, but wanted to smoke first. Wanna join me baby?" He smirked, scratching his shiny curly hair.

"No, honey, sit down so we can talk." I smiled even though I wanted to pounce on him and punch his face in. Brevin was three times my size though, so there was no way I would come out on top.

"Is everything good?" He walked over to me and leaned down to kiss me. I turned my head just in time for his lips to land on my cheek.

"Yeah, sit." I nudged him. "This big project came up and it's a great opportunity. The only thing is, Jadynn and I have to stay in Cincinnati where the event will be held."

"Damn, for how long? And what's the event for?"

"We're not sure yet, but for now it'll be just three weeks. And it's the same stuff as always, except we're umm, planning multiple high end events for this new venue to get them off the ground."

"Why did Eddie choose such a far city?"

"He didn't want to, but the place has a lot of potential. And the owner is paying top dollar for top PR service, so Eddie is sending his best people."

"Shit, well let me know what hotel you're gonna be at so I can come visit and shit."

"Sure, as soon as I find out I will let you know. But I have to pack right now and go meet Jadynn and Eddie at the car rental place. The whole trip is paid for."

"It better be," he sighed and looked off. "So when you get back we can start planning the wedding right?" He pulled me closer. "And we can start working on another baby. You've been healing this whole time but I miss you and that." He bit down on his lip, making me want to spit in his face.

I was so disgusted with myself and the things that I'd been putting up with from him. From turning a blind eye to his cheating, to allowing him to hit me whenever he got upset. I wished it didn't take another man to help me realize it, but I would never allow another human being to mistreat me the way I allowed Brevin to.

"Yeah we can work on all of that when I return." I patted his abs and backed away. His bare dick touching my clothes was repulsive to say the least.

"Okay," he gripped my face and forced his lips against mine, before turning away and walking to the bathroom for a shower.

While he cleaned up, I packed enough shit to last me for a month. I had everything I would need, including my favorite toiletries and jewelry. I planned never to sleep in this bedroom ever again.

As I walked towards the bedroom door to leave, I spotted blood on the wall and on the carpet from when Brevin killed our baby. He didn't even have it cleaned. I quickly dabbed my eyes with my wrist so that the tears sitting in them wouldn't fall and then left to head back to Teflon's.

Me: Everything went good. On my way. Hungry?

Teflon: Yeah, you want some chicken? I can stop at Popeye's.

Me: No, I will go to the store and cook for you.

Teflon: Aww shit, fasho.

I laughed at his text before locking my phone and pulling off. I couldn't wait to be completely free from Brevin.

***

"That chicken was good as fuck baby; I never had it spicy like that. Well not homemade at least." Teflon pecked me as soon as we laid down in the bed.

"Do you always give compliments like this? Or is this just beginning?" I giggled.

"I wouldn't call this giving you a compliment. I'm just speaking facts and shit. The chicken was good. It's rare that I get to eat homemade fried chicken."

"She didn't make it for you?"

"Yeah she did. She cooked for me every night, even the nights that I didn't come home." He spoke softly, as if he was reminiscing on his time with Kayla. I admit it made me feel a little bit uncomfortable because it seemed like he was maybe missing what he had with her. I liked him a lot, so I had to ask him.

"You miss that?"

"Home cooked meals on the daily?" He looked to me, letting his big hand grip my inner thigh. His touch always did something to me. It gave me a sense of safety.

"That and the chef." We chuckled in unison at my way of words.

"That's a tricky question honestly. I miss her, Kayla, the person she is, but I don't miss the relationship. Does that make sense?"

"Yes."

"Why'd you ask?"

"You just seemed to be traveling down memory lane for a little bit when I asked if she cooked for you. It made me wonder if you were regretting what we're trying to do here."

He turned on his side to face me and pulled my body closer into his. My hand naturally traveled down his rock hard abs, as I stared into his slanted eyes.

"No I was just thinking about how she did a lot for me, everything a man would want from his woman, yet I didn't feel the way about her that I feel about you."

"No matter how good a woman is, Teflon, if the guy isn't right it won't matter. Look at Brevin, he doesn't see me the way you see me."

"Very true." He nodded. "You're a fucking gem." He stared at me for a little longer and then asked, "What are you thinking about?"

"Nothing," I lied.

"Yeah you are. Whenever your eyes get all glazed over and your lips part a little bit, you're thinking deeply about some shit. I wanna know what it is."

"You pay such close attention to me," I whispered.

"I can't help it." He rubbed up and down my thighs. He was obsessed with them.

"I was just thinking that maybe all the stuff that happened in our previous relationships was because we were supposed to be with each other and not them."

"That's exactly what it is," he replied and I nodded. "How are you feeling?"

"Good." I smiled.

"No. I meant about the baby. You haven't said anything about it since it happened."

My smile immediately faded; I could feel it. Suddenly my mind became clouded with negative thoughts, wondering if I would ever have a baby. Delivering the last child was so traumatizing because it was basically for nothing. As soon as he came out, he was dead and it was over. I didn't realize my thoughts had produced tears until I felt Teflon brush them away and kiss me.

"We had a name for him and everything. I wonder if I'm ever gonna be a mother." I looked at his chest, admiring his tattoos.

"Hell yeah you will. The next time you get pregnant that shit is gonna be smooth sailing, trust me."

"How do you know?" I grinned since he was. I loved that he was so positive.

"Because it's gonna be mine and I'm gonna do everything in my power to make sure you and it are in perfect condition."

Pressing my lips against his, I lightly pushed him onto his back before removing my t-shirt and panties. His eyes wandered all over my body, enjoying every bit of it. Pushing his boxers down, his dick plopped right out, already hard as hell.

"You have a condom?" I quizzed.

"For what?" he frowned.

"The pull out method can only last for so long, Tef." I chuckled as he rubbed up and down my body with a lustful gaze.

He said nothing as he slightly lifted me and brought me down onto his dick. My body froze as he ripped me in two almost, filling my body up. He guided me up and down on his dick slowly, while letting his eyes prance all over my body. After finally adjusting to his size, I wound my hips, allowing the pleasure to fully take over.

"Damn, Tati," he groaned, gripping my small hips tightly in his hands.

I placed my hand onto his hard abs for leverage and continued to rock my hips while winding up and down on his pole.

"Mmm," my voice trembled as I felt my peak rising. I released, gushing on his pole as we both called out.

Flipping me onto my back while still inside of me, he crushed his lips against mine and tongued me down. As I hollered out, he bit down on my bottom lip while groping my thighs like always. I loved that he loved my body, every part of it, even if it wasn't that much.

"Fuck," he grunted, pounding into me while gripping my torso with his right hand. "Let me go Tati," he begged. I had my muscles tightened around his rod, because I knew I was about to cum again.

He kissed me nastily while thrusting into my center with force, before finally yanking out and cumming right on the sheets. He strategically moved me out of the way so that it wouldn't touch me and then scooped me up to take me to the bathroom. He cleaned his semen off before tossing the sheets into the washer and putting some new ones on. We showered together and then fell asleep in the warm bed cuddled up.

I loved being cooped up and away with him, but I knew it was simply the calm before the great storm.

CHAPTER SEVEN

Jadynn

One week later…

Tatiana's ass had me out in the open wearing shades, skullcaps, and tight knit buns to make sure I wasn't that recognizable. Brevin had niggas everywhere and if one of them saw me, her whole Cincinnati lie would be blown the fuck up. Usually this shit would irritate me, but I was happy she was figuring out a way to leave him. I wasn't quite sure of what the fuck her plan was since this trip was only gonna get her away from Brevin for three weeks, but she assured me that it was just the beginning.

Walking out of the doctor's office, I slipped my shades onto my face. I wasn't feeling well and just wanted to go home and relax. No one knew about what Russell had done to me, not even Tatiana. I wasn't ready to disclose something like that just yet because I was still mortified by it. I had nightmares a lot, almost every night, and every thump in my apartment had me on edge because I thought it was him. I even had to get my locks changed, regardless of the fact that Russell no longer had a key.

I was angry with myself for being with him for so long and allowing him to scar me both emotionally and now physically. I was so busy looking through the window at Tatiana and Brevin's relationship, that I didn't focus on my own enough to realize not only was Russell fucking around with my sister, but that he was clearly off his rocker. Yeah he didn't beat me throughout our relationship, but raping me trumped all of that.

My phone ringing pulled me from my thoughts and when I looked down I saw it was my sister Paige calling. I quickly hit ignore and then blocked her number right after. Before I could even crank my car up, my phone was going off again and when I saw my mother's face, I answered.

"Hey Ma."

"Hey, Jadynn. Why are you ignoring your sister?"

"What? Is she with you?"

"Answer my question."

"Ma, I'm ignoring her because she and I are no longer cool. I don't need you butting in and getting into this mess."

"You guys are my children so I'm going to butt in young lady. You need to come by and talk to her, Jadynn."

"You can forget about that."

"You need to quit being stubborn, that's why unfortunate things happen to you so much sweetie."

Shoving my tongue into my cheek to calm my irritation, I took a deep breath while closing my eyes. I usually wouldn't tell my mother the details of my problems, but since she wanted to be a fucking mediator, I was gonna let her have it all.

"Ma, instead of calling me, you need to talk to your daughter about sleeping with Russell." I held my breath almost, waiting for her to be just as floored as I was.

"So you're gonna let a man come in between you two?"

Wow, she knew.

"Wait a minute, so you knew about what she did and you still have the nerve to call me and reprimand me about not wanting to speak with her?"

"Jadynn how many times did you complain about that man? Do you honestly care that she's with him now? I mean, if you wanted him you sure had a strange way of showing it."

"Oh my gosh," I chuckled angrily. Paige had always been my mom's favorite so whatever she did, my mother would try to find a way to justify it. "You can't be serious right now, Ma."

"I am. If anything, this is a blessing in disguise. You didn't want Russell and clearly Russell didn't want you, so it all works out."

"Right, you sure know how to see the light in situations mother."

"Don't be sarcastic, Jadynn. Now come over here so you guys can talk this out. I made some blueberry cobbler, your favorite."

"On my way," I lied before hanging up.

I sat there staring out of my front windshield. A sharp pain shot through my chest and I just took a deep breath before pulling off.

The sun was starting to set and despite the dirty buildings I drove by, the city looked beautiful.

After stopping to get some things to make some simple chicken pasta with, I headed towards my house. As I parked, my phone rang and I looked down to see my new friend. A smile spread across my face uncontrollably, but I quickly wiped it before picking up.

"Hey friend," I giggled. I was so awkward.

"What's good homie? What are you doing?" his deep voice spilled through.

"I just got home. I was gonna cook some food and watch TV. Today's my last day off for awhile," I sighed, wondering how Tatiana and I were gonna discreetly work this party *in* town when we were supposedly *out* of town.

A lot of times we dealt with celebrities, so it was nothing for us to show up in the background of some paparazzi photos. And if Brevin found out, good Lord would that be an explosion.

"Just so happens I'm hungry as fuck. I'm tired of eating parfaits every night," he replied, making us both chuckle. He was hilarious, only because he didn't try to be and he was so weird, like me.

"I guess I could spare a plate of pasta and maybe seconds." I didn't realize I was smiling until I looked in my rearview mirror to smooth down my eyebrows.

"Aight, you live in downtown right?"

"Yeah, I will send you my address. Don't be stalking me though, Merce."

"I can't make any promises."

I just grinned while shaking my head before hanging up.

I hurried into my apartment and set everything down in the kitchen. I then rushed to take a shower, and once I was out, I put the pasta on. While letting the water come to a boil and letting the chicken finish baking, I spread lotion all over my body and put on some pajama shorts with a nice top. I wanted him to think I simply came home and changed my bottoms. I wasn't sure why I even showered and shit because he definitely wasn't getting any pussy.

By the time I started chopping up the baked chicken to mix in with the spinach and pasta, Merce was calling me to let me know he'd arrived. I text him my apartment number and then went back to cooking while waiting.

"It smells good as hell up in here and I ain't even no big fan of pasta."

He walked in dressed down in grey sweats, a hoodie, socks, and slide-ins. When he removed his jacket, I was a bit surprised because he wasn't as skinny as I had assumed. He had some muscle on him, not like a body builder, but I could definitely tell he worked out. The last time I saw him this dressed down, it was dark in his apartment so I couldn't really see in depth like now. His scent was natural but nice. I could tell he didn't drown himself in cologne before coming, but his soap definitely smelled good, either that or his deodorant.

"You gon' close the door or you waiting on someone else?" He broke me from my trance and I realized I was staring at him, holding the door open. I closed it.

Clearing my throat out of embarrassment I asked, "You're not a big fan of pasta? Then why did you come?"

"I mean I like pasta, but it ain't my favorite food or nothing." He leaned back on the couch and text something on his phone.

"Okay," I mumbled to myself. "What would you like to drink?" I quizzed.

"Anything is cool, nothing too fancy though," he replied, toying with one of my couch pillows.

I simply nodded and entered the kitchen to finish up the pasta. Once it was done, I piled the food onto the plates, placed them on the table, and got some cups. After everything was set, I sauntered into the living room to get him.

"It's ready if you want to come in here."

"You don't eat in front of the TV?" he frowned.

"No, not unless I don't have enough time to eat before a specific show comes on. Other than that, I eat in the kitchen. Eating in other areas of the house can bring bugs."

He nodded approvingly as if I'd just dropped some household knowledge on him.

We sat down at the table, and once we were situated, we began eating. I didn't notice we weren't talking until he spoke up.

"You good?"

"Yes, why wouldn't I be?"

"You ain't even eating the shit you cooked really. You're just staring at it like you're in deep thought."

"I wasn't in deep thought." I forced a laugh. I had been thinking, deeply, but he didn't know that and I definitely didn't want to talk about my thoughts.

"Yeah you were. One of your dimples in your cheek is always very pronounced when you're thinking." He stared me down while gulping some of the juice I'd poured him. I was learning that he was observant as hell.

"I promise I wasn't thinking," I continued to lie. Thank God he gave up, shrugging his shoulders before scarfing down the food.

When we were done, I cleaned our plates and went into the living room to see what he was watching. It appeared to be the movie *Juice* with Tupac and Omar Epps.

"Is this *Juice*?" I quizzed, sitting down next to him. I looked to the side of his face to see how into the movie he was. He was so handsome, even with his scruffy facial hair.

"Yeah it is. What you know about this?"

"Not anything actually. I've heard of it but I've never actually seen it really."

"Well get comfortable. It's good, I promise."

"I don't know if I can take your word for it, Merce." I chuckled, cutting the lamp off since it was giving me a slight headache.

"I have good taste." He looked to me with a serious expression and all I could do was nod.

Throughout the movie, we got more comfortable with one another as he explained certain things about the street life that I wasn't too aware of. I wasn't sheltered or anything, but I wasn't deep in the hood like he seemed to have been.

Anyway, I'd become so comfortable, that I was now lying in his lap as he played in my hair unknowingly. He smelled so fresh and I just loved the calmness of his scent. I could tell that I was in the presence of a man and not a little boy. It felt different and unfamiliar unfortunately, which explained the slight nervousness that had overcome me.

The movie appeared to be nearing the end, so it was quiet between us as the light from it flickered.

"Shit," I mumbled when I saw my mother calling. I was sure she was wondering why in the hell I hadn't showed up. I hit ignore and then tossed my phone onto the floor faced down.

"I'm guessing your mama pissed you off," he said in a low sexy tone.

"Yeah, but it's nothing new. She always takes up for my older sister Paige and this time I'm fed up with it."

"I know how that bullshit is."

"Your mother is the same?"

"My mother *and* father, actually. They feel like anything bad that happens to my little brother Sebastian is my fault. Even though the nigga is twenty-five years old, somehow I'm responsible for everything he does that's negative."

As I listened to him explain his situation with his brother, I realized we had a lot more in common than I thought. We were both the black sheep in a way.

"Hmm, your life sounds just like mine. Whatever Paige does, it's okay, but when I do something it's a problem. If we both do something, somehow I was the influencer even though I'm three years younger."

"How old is she?"

"She's twenty-eight, same age as you. I'm the same age as your brother." I chuckled. "Did he do anything recently? I remember you mentioning him in the bar both times we interacted."

"He got locked up back Los Angeles and I'm trying to build my cash flow to help him with that shit, you know? But my parents seem to think it's my fault that he got knocked and that I shouldn't have left the state, regardless of the fact that it was the only way for me to get money."

Merce's parents were annoying the fuck out of me and I'd never even met their asses.

"What's your real name?"

"Calvin. Calvin Capers. Now what did your sister do?"

I Got Your Back ◆ *Teflon & Tatiana's Love Story*

CHAPTER SEVEN

Merce

$\mathcal{I}$ stared down at Jadynn lying in my lap, waiting for her to answer my question. Whatever her sister had done seemed to be bothering her and for some reason I wanted to be her shrink right now. Because honestly, telling someone outside of Teflon my problems with Sebastian and my parents, felt good and I wasn't even as bothered as she seemed to be.

"She…" her voice trailed off as she adjusted her body. "She slept with my boyfriend, well he's not my boyfriend anymore but he was."

"Damn what the fuck?" I frowned down at her as if she were her shady ass sister. I was still stroking her hair because it was soft as hell.

"Yeah, and they're together now."

"You miss him?" I swallowed the lump in my throat, hoping she said no strangely. She wasn't my bitch or anything, but I didn't want her missing her ex, especially not one that would do her dirty like that.

She shook her head no, brushing against my lap.

I was about to speak but she began softly crying. Turning her onto her back, I lifted her just enough so that I could hug her tightly. I'd never encountered some shit like this, because the bitches I had been fucking with, I'd never spent time talking to them for them to get emotional. And as far as Savannah, she wasn't really the type to cry. Jadynn was different though, softer, more feminine, and I liked that shit. If I wanted to date another *nigga* I would.

"Jadynn, calm down shorty. It's okay to say you miss that nigga, I ain't gonna trip," I said while still cradling her small frame as it jerked. I didn't know why I said what I said, but it seemed like the truth would relax her if she got it out.

"He raped me!" she sobbed into my chest, prompting me to stiffen up.

"What?" I yanked her from me and glared into her eyes while holding her shoulders in a tight grasp.

"He came over here, he was mad, and he threw me to the floor..." she began bawling to the point where she couldn't finish her sentence, so even though I wanted to press her for more details, I just brought her back into an embrace.

"What was his name?" I decided to ask once her violent crying got a little calmer.

"Russell. I was gonna forget about it, but I got pregnant and I had to get an abortion last week. My sister wouldn't care though, would she?"

My fucking ears were burning as she spilled more information. This nigga had me fucked up and he didn't even know me. And I shouldn't have cared but I did. Jadynn was obviously traumatized and

I didn't like that shit.

"What's his last name?"

"Why?" she sniffled, pulling back a little bit.

"I'm just curious."

"No, you're not just curious. I can't give you his name, because you're gonna do something to him. That's sweet but don't." Her voice was low and innocent, as she touched the side of my face with her soft ass hands that smelled like sugar and flowers… or something like that.

"Please, Jadynn."

"No my sister loves him and if he dies she'll go out of her mind, and then so will my mom and it'll just be a mess. And he's not worth it."

"I promise I won't kill him," I offered a forced smile. I wasn't gonna kill homie because I got paid to do that, but I was definitely gonna 'talk' to him.

"I know you think you'd be helping me, but you're doing enough right now."

We stared at one another for a few moments, before I kissed her lightly. I pecked her a couple more times, before our tongues came in contact. While holding her, my free hand groped her body, making sure to get a nice handful of her ass. She didn't have a huge one but it was enough for me to grip so I was with it.

As our kiss became hungrier, I let my hands travel up to grip her breasts, which I already knew weren't in a bra. Once I'd felt those up enough, I traveled down her body and into her shorts, touching between her legs, which made her jump.

"Would you like some wine? I have wine." She was holding my wrist in her hand, silently telling me not to go any further.

"Aight." I nodded, removing my hand from her bottoms.

She got out of my lap and made her way into the kitchen to get the drink. While she did that, I just scanned the room, hoping my dick went down soon. While doing so, I spotted a letter from a credit union that was addressed to a Russell Thorne. I checked to make sure she was still in the kitchen, then grabbed the letter, folded it in half, and slipped it into my pocket. I was gonna get at that nigga whether she wanted to help me do it or not.

***

In the middle of the night...

Jadynn and I were asleep in her bed; well she was because I was too anxious to go to sleep. I'd hit one of my boys up and asked if he knew who Russell Thorne was. He was one of them niggas that knew every damn body in Cleveland, as long as they didn't live in the super nice parts of town. Jadynn's place wasn't in the hood, but it wasn't the best area either.

Anyway, after telling him I needed more information on Russell Thorne who used to fuck with Jadynn, he let me know that the nigga had gotten a job working for Target overnight. He claimed his shift was anywhere between 12am and 3am, because that's when niggas saw him pulling up to Target usually.

Slipping out of the bed quietly, I grabbed my jeans and slipped them up. My dick was going through it being next to Jadynn, especially when she would move and press her body up against mine. I wanted to smash too damn bad. You'd think a nigga hadn't had any pussy in forever.

Once I was dressed, I left out of her spot, headed to the Target on W 117th to get at this nigga. When I pulled up, I thought I saw him sitting on the bench outside, eating a sandwich, but since I wasn't sure of his features, I checked my phone once more. After comparing the photo sent to me by the homie, to the nigga sitting there looking like he wanted to kill himself, I came to the conclusion that it was him. Getting out of the car, I tucked my gun in my waist. I hadn't planned on using it, but you never know.

"What's good?" I spoke to him as I sat at the other end of the bench.

"Sup," he responded dryly while scanning his pathetic sandwich before taking another bite.

"Are you Russell Thorne?" I raised a brow.

"Who wants to know?" his face was balled up as he looked to me.

"Me nigga that's why the fuck I asked and judging by your reaction, you must be him," I low-key snapped even though I was trying to stay calm. Just thinking about the shit he'd done to Jadynn had me angry as hell all over again.

"Aye man, I don't know what the fuck your problem is, but there is no reason you should be looking for me. I don't even know you and whoever sent you, I don't know them either."

"Nah you're probably right," I nodded. "I just heard some shit about you that I didn't like so I thought I'd come and holler at you." I had my hood on, making sure to shield my face from the obvious ass cameras outside of the place.

"You ain't heard shit—"

WHAM!

I stood to my feet and punched the shit out of him, causing him to drop his sandwich and spit blood.

"Nigga what the fuck is wrong—"

WHAM!

I hit his ass again and after gaining some of his composure, he rose to his feet like he was about to do some shit. Before he could even swing, I hit his ass again making him collapse to the floor. The beating continued as I kicked and punched on his ass like he wasn't shit… he wasn't shit.

"The fuck—ah! Yo!" he yelled all kinds of incomplete sentences as I went in on his ass. When I felt like I'd finally had enough, I stood up straight and stared down at his beaten body and face. He looked up at me with his one good eye as I grimaced at him.

"Leave her alone," I gritted.

He was confused at first, but when his crinkled brows returned to their original place, I knew he understood exactly what the fuck I was talking about.

"Ah!" he cried out when I kicked him again. I flashed him my gun by lifting my shirt, before backing away and running off to my car.

I was thankful that when I got back to Jadynn's she was still asleep, because I'd taken her keys in order to be able to get back into her crib. After removing my clothing, excluding my t-shirt, socks, and boxers, I climbed back into the bed and slept like a baby. I needed that.

CHAPTER EIGHT

Tatiana

Teflon, Merce, and I were sitting in Teflon's living room, discussing what our plan was gonna be. I had two more days left on my *business trip* and Brevin was gonna be expecting me once they were over.

I wasn't sure how this was gonna work, because it didn't seem like Teflon had been doing much but making weird phone calls and spending time with me. Don't get me wrong, I loved being up under him and vice versa, but I wanted to make sure that he and I would end up together and not be ripped apart by Brevin and his people.

"Tef, man she has to play the part, that's the only way," Merce explained. He was sitting in the La-Z-Boy chair, while Teflon and I sat on the couch. I was hugging Teflon's muscular bicep while resting my chin on his shoulder and admiring his handsome side profile.

"There has got to be another way." He stared down at the floor in deep thought.

"It's really not man. Brevin is gonna be looking for her and she has to go home to him or he's gonna get suspicious."

"I don't want her in the house with that nigga, especially not alone. Nah, if she goes back to him for play, then so do we."

"What do you mean?" I leaned down to look into his face. His already slanted eyes were squinted as he stroked his beard.

"What I mean is Merce and I will figure out a way to work for his ass again and get back into his house. That way I can keep an eye on his ass, while working him over," Teflon explained.

"Aye I'm with that. He'll think everything is good and the whole time we'll be waiting to pull the rug from under him." Merce leaned up and nodded at Teflon with a smile.

"Then it's settled. I'm gonna hit up Groove and let him know that I thought about what he said, and I'm willing to come back and work for Brevin."

"Wait he asked?" Merce squinted his eyes.

"Basically. Groove told me that Brevin still needed some people, niggas like you and me, and said that Brevin was open to it being us."

"Are you sure?" I chimed in. Brevin was not the forgiving type, and with the way Teflon fucked him up, I couldn't see him willing to call it water under the bridge just yet.

"Yeah, I'm sure. Groove is my cousin before anything, so he wouldn't be telling me some shit if it weren't true. And he especially wouldn't tell me to set me up or some shit." Teflon pulled a blunt from this box holding a bunch of pre rolled ones and lit it.

Merce grabbed a blunt from the box and did the same, before

both guys rested and smoked. I sat there, wondering if this shit was gonna work. I had faith in my man, but I also knew that Brevin was nothing nice. However, he was only as tough as his men were so if anything Teflon and Merce needed to get at them first.

Around 11:45pm that night...

"Mmm, ahhh!" I called out as Teflon rammed into me from behind while holding my hair.

I had no choice but to grip the sheets and bite down on my lip so that I wouldn't wake all of Cleveland. He was so far inside of me, hitting every single spot that I was sure that I was about to be speaking in tongues. Reaching around the front of me, he spread my legs wider and forced my face back into the pillow. He then gripped my hips, pounding into me as he began to call out himself.

"Tatiiiii shit!" He grumbled just the way I liked.

You could hear our skin smacking together throughout his whole apartment, along with our loud moans. My juices spilled over and since this was about the fifth time releasing, my inner thighs were now wet. Yanking me up by my hair, he bit down on my shoulder and began to suck hungrily while winding his hips into me. I just whimpered, because I was close as hell to tapping out.

"You're so little but so sexy," he groaned in my ear before sucking it. Throwing me back down, he started beating it up doggy-style, while grasping my torso. "Look at you taking this dick," he moaned.

A few moments later, I was releasing again and he was spilling inside of me. We sat in the same position, panting like thirsty dogs for a second, before he slid out of me and planted the most sensual kiss on my lower lips from behind. It was so slow and deep that it made me shiver.

I turned on my back and collapsed as he went to the bathroom to grab some warm wet towels. He returned and cleaned me, which I thought was so sweet of him. He then used his towel to get himself right, before climbing into the bed with me. He kissed me gently, before going in with a little more passion and pulling away.

This 'business trip' was the shit.

***

Jadynn and I were eating lunch at the Blue Point Grill. We hadn't had time to just chill and eat in a long time. I was in the hospital after miscarrying and then kind of went right into hiding with Teflon. As far as her, she was being a little bit distant during that time, but I was dealing with my own shit so I didn't really take the time out to see why.

"Have you talked to Paige?" I got right to it because that was what I'd been wondering. I couldn't believe her ass had been sleeping with Russell. She was always jealous of Jadynn and me too I felt, but I never thought she would stoop so low.

"Hell no. She tries to call or text me here and there, but I ignore her ass every time. I just can't see our relationship returning to what it used to be."

"I can't blame you." I sipped my drink. "So I have to tell you something."

"What?"

"Teflon and I are kind of a thing."

"Umm, I knew that shit already. That nigga has had his eyes on you since he first met you Tatiana. And the way he stuck by you in the hospital, come on now. It's always been so obvious."

"It has?" I smirked because hearing this was flattering.

"Yeah it has! The first day I met him when we were having breakfast together, he just stared at you the whole time, no matter what, even when I was talking. It may have been love at first sight. But what about Brevin? How is that working out?"

Jadynn and I had been away from one another for too long. I mean we'd seen each other while working, but we couldn't exactly take that time to discuss anything. We'd texted one another certain details that were happening, like me catching Gloria and Brevin together, but nothing else really.

"Well Merce and Teflon have a plan for that and somehow he and I will end up together, meanwhile Brevin will just kind of go away."

I noticed when I mentioned Merce, her body language changed.

"How is that possible?"

"I don't know, but I trust them both. What do you think of Merce?" I decided to fish.

"He's umm, he's very…" She began grinning and chuckling when I cocked my head at her ass. "Okay we've been chilling but nothing more. We kissed though and shit almost started popping but no."

"Why'd you stop it?"

"Tatiana!"

"What? I wanna know! When Teflon kissed me my legs just parted for him."

"'Cause you're a hoe," she giggled. "But no, I had to get an abortion Tati." Her facial expression changed. "It was Russell's."

"What? When? Why didn't you tell me?" I couldn't believe my best friend was going through all of this shit while I was laid up getting sexed.

"Because I didn't think you would approve after what happened to you."

"Why did you sleep with Russell after what he did Jadynn?"

"I didn't want to Tatiana, he just did it, and then he left." She shrugged one shoulder as if it were nothing, but I could see in her face that she was bothered by it.

"Jadynn, you need to tell somebody or something!" I yelled louder than I'd intended to. I was floored right now and felt like killing Russell. I may have been small but maybe I could still knock his ass around. Rage gave you strength at times.

"Relax Tati, I'm okay now. I'm really trying to forget about it, which is why I don't talk about it nor do I try to think about it. You're my best friend and I'm looking for you to make me feel better and to keep my mind off of it."

As much as I wanted to continue grilling her and figuring out why the fuck Russell hadn't had a hit put out on him, I dropped it. I knew too well how easy it was to just push a traumatizing experience to the back of your mind. I hated to talk about losing my last baby, so I'm sure this subject was sensitive for her as well.

"Fine. But if you ever wanna call a hitman, let me know." I smirked, making her laugh. I loved to see her smile, especially after witnessing how hurt she was from what Russell and Paige had done.

"I will. But tell me how is Teflon in bed?" her eyes bucked. Jadynn was always like this. When I lost my virginity to Brevin, she literally made me call her right after and explain how it went.

"He's very versatile, meaning he knows how to make love to me, but then he can turn right around and fuck me like a streetwalker," I explained and chuckled at the fact that her jaw was on the table damn near. She kept her surprised expression on as the waiter set down our plates.

"Girrrrl, that's my type of nigga! What about head?"

"Hell yeah! He was all in there. I told him he didn't have to the first time, but he insisted." I shrugged.

"Fuck did you tell him he didn't have to for? You know that's a requirement!"

"It is, but I was referring to that time in particular since technically I was still Brevin's woman. I guess right now I still am in his eyes," I nibbled on my lip as I thought about the fact that I would have to return home to him tomorrow.

"Yeah, Teflon is gonna be sick."

"I know but he doesn't need to worry, I won't be sleeping with Brevin."

"Good luck pulling that off. Hopefully he will be too busy smashing Gloria to even care," she reminded me of his affair.

"Yeah," I sighed, shaking my head.

For the first time in my life, I was praying that Brevin had some other females to keep his dick company, because I surely didn't plan on satisfying him in the bedroom.

CHAPTER EIGHT

Teflon

I was sitting on the passenger side of Groove's car, staring out at my hometown as he headed towards Brevin's crib in Ohio City. The mere thought of Brevin made my skin crawl, but I needed to get that shit under control if I was gonna be working for him.

"Remember Tef, you gotta be cool so he will accept the idea." Groove turned his music down.

"What? I thought you said it was his idea to have Merce and I back. I didn't know I was gonna be coming here to plead for this muthafucka's forgiveness!" I barked. I wanted to knock the shit out of this nigga.

"Yeah, what the fuck is you talking about, Groove?" Merce questioned from the back seat.

"Look he was all for Merce coming back on the team, but you Teflon, not so much. But can you blame him? You whooped his ass in his own house!"

"Because he was beating the shit out of his girl!"

"Is that really why, Tef? Or is it because you were interested in her."

"Man." I sucked my teeth.

Yeah I wanted Tatiana at the time, but if Groove thought I was the type of nigga to sit around while niggas smacked on their women he was crazy. And it wasn't like he was just slapping her, he was for real fighting her little ass, so regardless of whether I wanted her or not, I would have jumped in.

"Teflon, do you want her as yours?" he finally asked as he pulled up in front of Brevin's crib. Because Groove was my cousin, Merce and I let him know the real reason I was agreeing to come back. And since I was his family, he was rocking with me.

"He does," Merce answered for me.

"I know you do and she's more important than this beef, right? Getting paid is more important than this beef, right? Just make amends with the nigga to save your girl. If you go in there and piss him off, he's not gonna let you back on and he'll be able to keep Tatiana."

"I would just kill his ass."

"Okay and then what happens when his people come after you and/or us?"

"I'll kill their asses too."

"Yeah maybe some of them but not all of them, Tef. Just game this nigga up and snatch his empire and his girl."

I nodded slowly after staring at his home for a minute. She was in there with him and that shit bothered me like crazy. Groove was right though, starting shit with this nigga when I didn't have the army to get Tatiana was stupid. I needed to bite the bullet and play nice if I wanted my girl and if I wanted to get paid.

The only thing that may be a problem was that I wasn't used to faking it with niggas. I was always very blunt and spoke my mind, so having to smile in this hoe ass nigga's face was gonna do some terrible shit to my spirit. However, Tatiana was worth it. If that nigga Jack from Titanic could freeze to death for his bitch, I could surely do something as small as playing a role for mine.

"Come on," I finally said, pulling my hood onto my head and exiting the vehicle.

The three of us made our way up the walkway, and Merce and I waited behind Groove as he rang the doorbell. I closed my eyes to say a silent prayer and right when I was done the door opened. Tatiana stood there in some little ass shorts that I didn't approve of while she was here and a bikini bra. I got mad all over again, wondering if she'd let this nigga fuck last night. We made eye contact and right when she gave me that pretty ass smile Brevin came and stood next to her in the doorway, kissing her lips. I just clenched my teeth and glanced off for a second.

"Groove man, what the fuck? I just said Merce," he grimaced.

I simply chuckled and shook my head as Groove explained why we both were here. *Calm down man*, I told myself as I shoved my hands into my pockets.

Brevin just smacked his lips after Groove elaborated and then walked into the house. We followed him in and Groove went back to close the door since I'd left that shit open. Fuck him and his house.

We made it to the den and after taking a seat, Tatiana brought us drinks just like last time. When she handed me mine, I looked intently into her eyes, to which she offered a soft subtle smile in response. I didn't like this shit at fucking all. She was my *girl* not this nigga's. And just the thought of him fucking her last night, had my hands itching to punch him.

"So talk!" Brevin snapped once she left.

"Things got out of hand the last time man and I guess I just reacted as a reflex. I'm not used to seeing niggas hit their woman like that," I stated.

"Tatiana is my woman, meaning what goes on between her and I is no one's business, especially not some nigga who works for me."

I simply grinned at him, ready to fuck him up. Groove could see it so he cleared his throat to begin speaking.

"And Teflon understands that, which is why we're here. We all wanna put this behind us and move forward. You need the protection right now Brevin, and badly. Niggas ain't fucking with you, especially now that the streets have been dry due to your personal issues," Groove said.

Brevin stared down at the floor, pondering, before finally picking his head back up and nodding. We went over pretty much the same details and agreed that Merce and I would accompany him if it was a big event only, but only one of us needed to trail him if it was something small. Also, we would take out anyone he directed us to, and my favorite part of the whole deal is that we'd be living here. Groove knew that was my only stipulation and Merce agreed to keep the fact that we had our own spots a secret.

Game time.

✳✳✳

That night…

"I just came to see if you were comfortable," Tatiana peeked her head into the room smiling. She still had on that short and bra ensemble that I didn't approve of. She wasn't voluptuous but she was still sexy and I knew I wasn't the only one who thought so, which is why I didn't like that outfit.

"Come in here and close the door."

"Tef, he's up there sleeping."

I didn't respond, I just stared at her. She came in like I'd asked and closed the door behind herself. I watched her as she made her way over to me in the bed. I was ass naked, ready to get it in, but she didn't know that yet. As soon as she got close, I sat up and pulled her closer to unbutton her shorts.

"Tef are you crazy!" she shouted in a whisper.

I just pecked her and pushed her shorts down her little frame until they hit her ankles. I did the same to her underwear while sucking and kissing on her neck and collarbone making her moan softly. She smelled so good and her skin was like soft caramel. Reaching behind her, I loosened the bikini top and threw it to the side. I trailed my pointer finger across her body as my eyes followed, just admiring.

"You slept with him?"

"No, I told you I wouldn't," she replied as I gripped her and threw her down on the bed.

"Nah, sit on my face." Yep I was about to be doing the most in this nigga's house. She bucked her eyes, so I tugged on her arm so that she'd sit up.

Lying back, I waited as she mounted my face and brought her pussy to my mouth. I palmed her small round ass as I kissed and licked between her hips for a little bit. Her body quivered as stuttered moans burst through. I could tell she was trying to muffle them to the best of her ability.

Pushing her pussy down more into my mouth so that I could attack her clit, I moved her back and forth to let her know I wanted her to ride. She caught on quickly, leaning forward to use my abs for leverage as she wound her hips against my face, putting her shit all in my mouth. She was so wet you could literally hear me eating her pussy. I was in pussy eating heaven right now.

"Mmmm, Tef, oh, oh my go—" her body trembled when she released into my mouth. I just lapped it up and kept sucking her clit, enjoying the sound of her moans.

She came again and I just swiftly put her on all fours. Pushing her face into the bed, I wiggled my way inside of her tight walls and immediately started beating it up. I smiled watching her hands grasp the sheets as she cried out.

"Is this my pussy, Tati?" I groaned, pounding into her. She was sopping wet, making it hard for me not to call out like a bitch.

"Yes, Tef it's yours. Yes," she whimpered, placing her little hand behind herself to touch on my abs. I quickly moved it, because she wasn't about to be running shit.

She began crying out with every deep stroke I delivered, so I pulled her arms behind her back to hold them while I fucked the shit out of her, making her cum hard. Damn. Her pussy deserved a fucking award on everything I loved. The sound of me beating it up was my favorite damn song right now. All you could hear was her moaning and my dick slamming into her tight wet walls.

"Fuck," I grumbled, knowing I would be cumming soon.

I yanked her body into mine and craned my neck around to suck and bite her nipples. I kept stroking her, but much slower as I vacuumed her nipple into my mouth. Her body was drenched in sweat, as I ran my hand down the front of her to toy with her clit.

"Tef," she sniveled.

I placed her on her back and then put her legs onto my shoulders. My dick was so hard I didn't need to guide it in. As soon as I came in contact with her opening, I pushed myself inside. We both let out a loud moan when that happened.

"You feel so fucking good!" I growled as I moved in and out of her slowly. She was flexible as fuck because I had her legs up and she didn't move them. "Lick your lips like that again," I demanded. I loved when she did that shit.

She licked them just before I let one of her legs down to kiss her passionately, while still sliding in and out of her with precision. Realizing I didn't have much stamina left, I put her leg back on my shoulder and began pounding her middle with force. She was damn near screaming by this time, but that shit was too sexy to care if anyone heard. I too was moaning by now as I beat it up with the perfect pace. After a few minutes of that euphoria, we both called out, releasing.

I let her legs down so that I could kiss her deeply and she locked them around my waist while caressing the side of my face. We laid there like that for an eternity it seemed until we passed out.

Around 3am, she shook me to let me know she was gonna go back upstairs to be with him. I kissed her as if I thought I would never see her ass again and then let her go. I stared at the door for a few moments after it was closed as if she were still standing there. I wasn't sure if I could do this shit.

CHAPTER EIGHT

Jadynn

"Ma, what was so important that you needed to get me over here," I sighed, plopping down on her couch. She promised me that it'd be just her and I and since I stood her up last time I decided to come.

Before I could finish folding my arms, out walked Paige with a fucked up Russell. I snapped my neck to look over at my mother and she placed her hand on my arm to stop me from getting up. I looked back to Russell's face and cringed at the sight. Whomever he fought knocked the dog shit out of this nigga, and trust me he was filled with plenty of dog shit.

"Was it this serious, Jadynn?" My mother pointed to Russell, who couldn't even look at me. Paige was rubbing his back as if he was the love of her life. I couldn't believe she thought it was okay to show affection to him as if just months ago he wasn't my man.

"I don't know what you're talking about Ma, but I'm about to leave."

"You had him beat up you jealous bitch!" Paige yelled.

"I'm jealous? How the fuck can you call me jealous when you spent years trying to get me to break up with him so you could have him!"

"I spent years telling you to leave him because I cared about you! I knew he loved me and I thought it was best for you to dump him before you found out Jadynn!"

"Are you serious right now? You care about me, yet you slept with my man and are now in a relationship with him." I squinted my eyes in confusion at her.

"Yes I'm serious! And there was no need to have him mutilated like this, just because he doesn't want you! There are plenty of men in this world, Jadynn."

She had to have been joking. If there were so many men in the world, why did she come for mine? But like my mother said, this was a blessing in disguise. Who knows when I would have gotten rid of Russell, had I not caught his dick in Paige's mouth?

"You know what? I don't even care anymore. I don't know how he got like that, but it serves him right."

"The nigga told me to leave you alone, so I know you sent him!" Russell finally made a peep.

"What—" I stopped short when I remembered the fire of wrath burning inside of Merce's eyes when I told him what Russell had done to me. I was angry with him for going behind my back, but I would be straight up lying if I didn't say I was happy to see Russell had been punished for what he'd done.

"Yeah, now you recall, huh hater?" Paige pulled me from my

thoughts.

"Jadynn I'm appalled. I didn't want to believe you had anything to do with this, but I see I was wrong and your sister was right. You didn't even want Russell, so why go to such extremes?" My mother balled up her beautiful yet aged face.

"Maybe if he hadn't barged into my house and raped me, this wouldn't have happened to him." Both my sister and mother gasped, as Russell shot daggers at me. "Yeah, your boyfriend raped me, got me pregnant, and I aborted it. So am I sorry that he got fucked up? No." I grabbed my purse and started out, but someone grabbed me. When I turned around to see it was Paige, I couldn't help myself.

WHAM!

I punched her and she flew back. Straddling her, I began raining blows all over her face as my mother attempted to pull me off her. Russell stood there, yelling some bullshit, but not touching me. I guess he was scared Merce would come after him again if he did.

"Stop Jadynn, please!" my mother screeched as I pummeled Paige's face.

Tired of my mom running around like a chicken with its head cut off, I got off of a crying and bloody Paige and left out.

All three of them could go suck a fat one.

***

"You missed me?" Merce stood in my doorway smiling and looking sexy as ever.

Have you ever realized that the more you saw a person, the more attractive they became? That's how it was with Merce. Right now, he was the finest nigga in Cleveland… shit Ohio.

"Come in," I responded dryly.

"Damn, some kind of welcome. Aye you got a bottle opener for this shit. It's supposed to be some good ass wine and I thought I'd try it with you, my best friend." He chuckled in his deep raspy voice as he began rumbling through my kitchen.

"Calvin, why did you beat up Russell?"

"Calvin? Damn," he laughed as he put the bottle opener down. "I didn't know I couldn't." He shrugged.

"I told you to leave him alone!"

"No, you said not to kill him and so I didn't, I just whooped his ass." He gulped some of the wine straight from the bottle. "This shit is good, want some?"

"I wanted you to leave it alone."

"Why? That nigga busted off in your house and took advantage of you! If you're not gonna report the shit to the police, at least let him pay for it another way!"

"Merce—"

"Jadynn, I like you and I'm not the type of nigga to sit around and let you have problems of your own to deal with. I know you're a strong black woman and all that shit, but he needed to be taught a fucking lesson. As long as I'm alive, no nigga is gonna disrespect you and if he does then he'll get the same treatment Russell got, maybe worse."

I couldn't even be mad at him, because I understood where he was coming from. You get so used to being around bitch ass niggas who are too scared to take up for you, that it's weird to come in contact with a no nonsense type. Merce was a thug ass nigga and not the fake type like Brevin and Mack. I guess I would have to get used to that if we were going to continue to be friends.

"Fine." I smirked and walked up closely to him. I inhaled his scent that I enjoyed so much and tilted my head back to look up into his rugged but handsome face.

He kissed me, while wrapping his long muscular arm around my waist. I'd never dated a nigga as tall as him.

"How did you know I beat him up? He called you crying?"

"No," I giggled. "I went over to my mom's house and she had him and my sister there to confront me. I ended up beating her ass."

As soon as I finished we both burst into laughter.

"See we really are best friends." He grinned and so did I.

"I guess so."

After drinking the wine, we ordered some delivery Chinese food, and just pigged out and watched movies. I liked that he made moves on me, but they were subtle ones. He would touch me in intimate areas like my inner thigh, or peck me, but he never did too much. Not that I wasn't all for fucking him because I was, but right now I wasn't ready and I could tell he knew that. I liked having him as a friend, but I admit I didn't want any other girls being his associate at this point.

CHAPTER EIGHT

Merce

I was in this big ass bedroom at Brevin's house smoking a blunt. Last night that nigga wanted to go out, so Teflon and I had to come out with him. We weren't feeling the idea at first, but that shit got wild and was hella fun. We had all kinds of fucking liquor and champagne being passed around that shit and plenty of hoes to choose from too. And for the first time, neither Teflon nor I were touching any of them females. I knew Jadynn wasn't my girl, but I wasn't touching them because I just wasn't interested. I couldn't get Jadynn off of my mind for shit, so another girl couldn't do anything for me right now.

As I ashed the blunt getting ready to go to the bathroom to brush my teeth, my phone rang. I looked down to see it was my little brother calling which was odd. That nigga was in jail so I wasn't sure why someone was hitting me from his cellphone.

"Hello?" I answered, frowning like fuck in the mirror as I pulled down my mouthwash and shit.

"Merce, what's up man?"

"Sebastian? How the fuck are you calling me from a damn cellphone?"

"I'm out man, umm, I need you to get me a plane ticket out to Cleveland."

"Out? How the hell did you get out already? Them niggas said you'd be in for three years and I haven't even secured the lawyer yet."

Don't get me wrong, I was happy that my little brother was out of jail, but I was confused. I'd just gotten in contact with a lawyer and he told me it'd cost me about $100,000 because of Sebastian's record. Teflon and I handled a couple jobs before Brevin fired us and we also did one this week, so I was solid as fuck. All I planned to do was meet up with the lawyer and pay him the first installment he requested, but it looked like I wouldn't have to.

"That nigga that you used to work for? Luis? His brother got me out."

I stared blankly into the mirror as I processed what the fuck he'd said. I knew deep down that Diego had done this shit not to help me, but because he had an ulterior motive.

"Aight umm, look I'm gonna buy you a ticket for tomorrow morning, Bash. Do not tell anyone that you're leaving the state, not even the nigga that got you out."

"Well I got you on speaker and Will can hear you."

I balled my fist up, clenched my teeth, and closed my eyes so that I wouldn't call this nigga every insulting name that there was. My brother was dumb as a box of fucking rocks sometimes, so it was good that he was bringing his ass back to Cleveland. I planned to drop his ass right off to my parents so they could deal with him. No longer would I be getting blamed for the bullshit he liked to pull.

"Take me off speakerphone, Sebastian," I gritted as calmly as I could.

"Aight. So when should I look for the ticket Merce?"

"In like twenty minutes. Text me your email. And Bash, if you don't make this fucking flight you're gonna have to call Mom or Dad to fly you out."

"I'm gonna make the flight Merce damn," he sucked his teeth.

"Bye."

I hung up before he could say anything and then proceeded to brush my teeth. After flossing and rinsing, I turned the shower on and did a good ass scrub down.

The whole time I was wondering why in the hell Diego did what he did. I hoped he wasn't salty about the fact that Teflon and I decided to leave instead of continuing to work with him. Shit, who was I kidding? He was definitely pissed about that shit because he'd said it. Fuck! I hated being in the dark about people's moves.

I stepped out of the bathroom after drying off and grabbed some boxers to slip on before getting dressed. After putting on a little bit of my cologne, I was out the door and heading to pick Jadynn up for lunch. I told her she could pick anywhere to eat and I was hoping she didn't choose a place that was like $400 a plate. I had it, best believe I did, but I just wasn't trying to blow a grand on dinner.

We ended up at this place named Dante, in Tremont and it was a pretty cool looking spot. I could tell it was pricey, but it was the reasonable kind not like what I'd mentioned earlier.

"Have you eaten here before?" I furrowed my brows as I scanned the menu for something interesting.

"No, this would be the first time." She gave me that sexy ass smile that made her dimples appear in both cheeks.

"Oh so you chose this place for me to take you to, to spend all my damn money? Okay cool." I nodded and she laughed.

"No, I've just wanted to come here for a while and since you said to pick anywhere, I did."

"Right."

The waiter approached the table to take our drink orders. I got beer and water, and Jadynn got some frilly ass martini. The waitress returned about twenty minutes later for our food orders, and once she was done she turned to walk away, but then swirled right back around.

"Aren't you Savannah's boyfriend?" the waitress asked, hand on her hip like if I said yes she was gonna do something.

"Nah, I'm not anybody's boyfriend. But keep it professional aight?"

She glanced at Jadynn and then nodded before leaving the table.

"Savannah, that's the ex you told me about?"

"Yeah. I told you she ain't my ex though, because she was never my girlfriend."

"Have you seen her recently?"

"I have since I've been to Cleveland yes, but not lately. But let's change the subject baby; I really don't want anybody else to be our topic of conversation."

"Okay." She nodded. "Why is your nickname, Merce?" she cocked her head and squinted her eyes.

"Because Teflon and I used to get into fights with niggas all the time and people would say that I beat niggas up mercilessly. And people started calling Tre'Wayne, Teflon because he's a resilient ass nigga. Like he will go through shit that would break most people but he always perseveres. And he never let's that shit change him. So this old nigga in the hood named Walt started calling him Teflon, because he said that was a tough ass material used as a barrier to block shit out."

"Wow," she cheesed. "Most niggas have nicknames that are dumb as fuck, but you guys' have some sense to them. And I definitely agree on the reason why they call you Merce. And Groove?"

"He can dance real good." I chuckled at the thought.

"Really?" she laughed. "Like Chris Brown good or he can just stay on beat."

"Nah like CB," I laughed only because she did. I loved seeing her crack up.

"I just can't imagine him doing all that, but I hope to witness it one day." She nodded with a half smile, still snickering lightly.

We talked some more until our steaks came. After tearing those down, we got dessert. The food was good as hell for sure, but those damn portions were weak as fuck.

We left the restaurant and headed to my spot to just chill. I explained to her that this place was to be kept a secret now, because we didn't need Brevin finding out.

I opened some champagne for the two of us and grabbed two glasses before joining her on the living room floor. She loved sitting on the floor for some reason, and since my spot was facing the water, she loved looking out of the window.

"What you thinking about?" I asked as I sat next to her, handing over the glass to fill it up.

"Just life. What are you thinking about?" She looked to me, letting her eyes dance all over my face like always.

"You."

"Yeah?" she raised a brow before setting her flute down next to her.

I simply nodded as I watched her pull her dress over her head. A nigga was stuck, just taking in her sexy ass frame for a second.

Tossing back the rest of my champagne, I pulled her into my lap so that she was straddling me and unhooked her bra as I sucked on her lips. I gazed at her breasts once they were revealed before cupping them to suck on her nipples. She threw her head back in ecstasy, grinding her hips in my lap very subtly.

"No let's do it here, by the window," she suggested when she saw I was about to carry her to my bedroom. Shit, I was so hard right now, I didn't care where we did the shit. I'd fuck her on some train tracks right now.

I rose to my feet and so did she, helping me get out of my clothes. I did the same, removing only her panties since that was all she had left. Once we were both ass naked, I backed her into the window, and dropped down to place one of her legs onto my shoulder. I started off slowly, licking between her slit and flicking my tongue over her button. I did that for a little bit, then touched to see how wet she was and damn…

I lifted her so that both of her legs were on my shoulders and she gripped a portion of the windowsill as I sucked on her pussy like I was getting paid for it. Her coos and moans were soft and filled with pleasure as I massaged her thighs while sucking her clit.

"Calvin," she whimpered, massaging my fade as she released.

I buried my face deeper into her center, making love to it with my mouth, as her cries got louder. I felt her tremble again, this time more violently, so I let up.

Placing her to her feet gently, I made sure she didn't fall over as she got down on her knees. She took my dick into her warm mouth and I must admit getting head while looking out over the water was some fire ass shit.

Once I saw she was all into sucking me up, I began pumping slowly into her face. She was moving right along with me, at the perfect pace. Every time I pushed my dick into her mouth, she opened her throat letting my head bump her tonsils.

"Fuck," I groaned whenever I felt the back of her throat.

She sped up, letting her mouth become drenched while slurping me. I couldn't hold on anymore and let my first nut flow freely. I ain't know if she was the swallowing type, but she was sucking my dick so good that I didn't have the time to tell her I was busting. To my surprise she threw it back, so I yanked her up and kissed her for a little bit before getting a condom from my wallet. After rolling it down, I picked her up into my arms and brought her down onto my dick. It was a struggle at first, but after pressing her back into the window and pushing with all of my might, I made it inside of her.

"Damn," I grumbled. Even with the condom, her shit was off the chain.

As I pumped into her, I kissed on her neck while she caressed the back of my head. Holding her small thighs in my hands, I kept her legs open for more access, winding my hips into her.

"Uhhh, ahhh," she called out every time she hit the base of my dick. This fucking in the window shit was for real the business.

Gripping her tighter against my body, I began slamming into her while sucking her lips, letting her cry loudly into my mouth. This was the wettest pussy I'd ever had in my life and the feeling was phenomenal. I could feel my toes on the verge of curling every time I hit her ass deeply. Shit.

"I'm about to nut, Jay, shit!" I groaned into her mouth.

Her ass came as soon as I said that shit, making her pussy even wetter. This shit was too much for me right now. I swear if she gave this shit to another nigga I may want to kill his ass. I decided just to give up and began beating the pussy up making her yell out. She came one more time and right afterwards so did I. That was hands down the best nut I'd achieved in the longest.

I pulled out of her once I had enough strength to and carried her to the bathroom so we could clean up.

I definitely wasn't done with her sexy ass for the night though.

CHAPTER NINE

Tatiana

Tonight I was gonna cook some spicy fried chicken, because I knew Teflon loved it. He would know I made it for him and I loved that.

I must say I enjoyed sneaking around with him, because it made my orgasms that much greater. Letting him fuck me hard right under Brevin's nose got my adrenaline pumping. I couldn't wait until all this was over, but I also couldn't lie and say I wasn't enjoying it slightly.

Another good thing was that I think Brevin was scared to get rough with me while Teflon and Merce were there. There have been times where he usually would have slapped me around, but he refrained because Teflon or Merce were nearby. I appreciated the fear they put into his heart for sure.

After checking out at the grocery store, I pushed my basket to the car and began unloading everything. I felt a presence near me as I filled the trunk, so I stopped and turned to look at whom it was.

"Yes?" I looked at the girl standing next to me. She was wearing a really tight dress and her hair was disheveled. I could tell she'd been crying a little bit.

"Tell Brevin that I'm not getting rid of our baby and if he keeps ignoring me he and I are gonna have a problem."

"Baby?" I turned to face her fully.

"Yes *baby*. Since you're his fiancée and you're so close to him when he's not in my bed, tell him Amanda said the baby is here to stay."

"No he's *your* child's father so figure out a way to get in contact with him. I'm sure you can come up with something if you were smart enough to catch me at the grocery store."

She looked down at me frowning as if I were supposed to be scared. Yeah she was a good 5'7 and I was 5'1, but I wasn't scared of anybody. I would fight her ass and anybody else if they wanted it. I'm sure she expected me to hit her, but a part of me didn't even care about what Brevin had going on really. On the flip side though, this situation made me sick to my stomach, the fact that he was out here getting every damn body pregnant.

"Let him know my thirteen week check up is in a week," she added before turning on her heels and walking off.

Slamming my trunk closed, I hopped into my car and sped to the home that Brevin and I shared. I was gripping the damn steering wheel so tightly that my hands were red. When I pulled up to our home, I neglected to get the shit out of the trunk because it was the least of my worries right now.

I darted up the stairs and went into the bedroom to see if Brevin was in there. He'd usually be showering at this time because he stayed sleeping in late. When I got into the bedroom, I saw our housekeeper Suzanne placing some of his undergarments into his drawers.

"Good morning Ms. Drew, are you looking for Mr. Williamson?" She smiled that sweet smile of hers.

"Yes, I am. Do you know where he is?"

"Yes he's down in the den eating lunch with your houseguests."

"Thank you."

I left out of the bedroom and shuffled down the stairs. I was hitting them two at a damn time and not missing a beat even though I was short. Finally making it to the den, I spotted Brevin, Teflon, and Merce, chilling and eating a big plate of food. They were watching some shit on TV, while Brevin talked their ears off.

Teflon looked so handsome, even though he wasn't dressed up. He was in a simple pair of black jeans, a black thermal, and a black hat. His beautiful brown skin was so clear and supple and his facial hair was scruffy but neat. His beautiful slanted eyes just added to his sexy features. Somehow, I could smell his cologne the most, even though he was in a room with two other niggas that I knew wore a scent.

"Good morning fellas. Brevin, can I talk with you for a second?" I walked in, prompting all three guys to look my way.

I watched Teflon scan my frame while licking his full lips, before making his way back to my face. I loved that he made me feel like I was voluptuous and shit. I gave him a quick half smile before following Brevin out of the den and pulling him into the room next door.

"What's up, baby?" He smiled, pulling me into his strong grip.

"Brevin stop." I moved when he leaned down to kiss my neck. "Who the hell is Amanda?"

"Amanda?" he cocked his head, playing dumb. I knew Brevin like the back of my hand, so I could tell he was playing the part right now.

"Yes, Amanda! She told me she's having your fucking baby!" I found myself yelling when I didn't even mean to.

"She's lying Tati! You know all these bitches out here are on my damn dick shorty! Come on! Please tell me you don't believe that bullshit!"

"How can I not? You stay out all fucking night, you come home with lipstick prints on your fucking pants, and I saw that bitch text you before!"

I was piping hot by this time, as I remembered seeing Amanda text him a while back. Funny enough it was the same night he romanced me and all that bullshit.

"You ain't seen shit, Tatiana. You're fucking tripping right now. I don't know a bitch named Amanda and no girl is having my baby. You know I wouldn't get no other bitch pregnant, especially not after what happened to us."

"You're a fucking liar!" I shouted, punching him in the chest as tears started to develop. I thought I wouldn't care but it was getting to me.

"Baby, Tatiana!" he gripped me into his body as I attempted to try and hit him some more. He kissed my face as I sobbed into his chest. I couldn't believe he would do some shit like this to me.

"I'm gonna fix this okay?" he looked down into my face. "Don't cry baby, I'm gonna fix this. I haven't been with another girl since I cheated three years ago, I promise," he lied.

I knew he'd been fucking Gloria because I caught him and I knew Amanda wasn't lying. I hated that he could lie to my face so easily. Even his facial expression showed sincerity, but unfortunately for him I had evidence proving otherwise and I knew his tricks like the back of my damn hand.

Before I could say anything he kissed my lips and hugged me. He then left out of the room, snatching his keys from the bookshelf in the hallway. And just like that he was off somewhere.

I wiped my face and then walked out, bumping right into a fuming Teflon. He yanked me back into the room, and then locked the door behind himself.

"So that's what we're doing now?" he folded his strong arms across his chest. I could see his muscles under his thermal, even though it wasn't that tight.

"What are you talking about?"

"You in here crying over this nigga? For real, Tatiana? I could hear you in the den going off about him fucking another bitch!"

"No, I was going off because he got her pregnant!"

"So you care."

"Yes I care! He got her pregnant while I was lying in the hospital after losing our baby! Yes I care!" I screamed at him. Was he stupid or something? I'd been with Brevin half of my life damn near, so yes I was gonna be upset at the fact that he got another hoe pregnant while I was recovering from losing our baby.

Teflon just nodded slowly before glancing off for a few seconds.

"So be with him then," he spoke calmly and dryly. I didn't like his tone at all.

"I don't want to be with—" I stepped closer to him but he backed up.

"Nah I think you do. Look at you. You're messed up over the fact that he got another woman pregnant. So since you love him you need to be with him." He turned to leave.

"Tre'Wayne!"

"Nah. I ain't gon' even trip off you. You love him so do what you want. But I'm done playing games so I wish you and him the best of luck on your impending nuptials."

"Tre'Wayne!" I called after him again as he left out of the room. I followed him out and when I finally caught up to him I grabbed the back of his shirt.

"Get the fuck off me, Tatiana!" he turned to me and roared, making me jump. "I'm done with you! From now on don't fucking talk to me or any damn thing! This is a wrap! I'm sick of your back and forth bullshit so be with that nigga! I'm begging you!"

Before I could respond, he left. Tears started to stream my cheeks. When I turned around, I saw Merce there, looking at me with pity. I started to break down, and he just pulled me into a hug to calm me.

"He's in love with you shorty, that's all," Merce whispered as he rubbed my back.

This was all becoming too much.

CHAPTER NINE

Teflon

That night…

Brevin, Groove, Merce, and I all sat in this secluded area of the strip club. The women here were beautiful and even had the bodies to match, which was a first. Usually if the girl was pretty her body was weak and vice versa, but tonight 90% of them were on point.

However, the only thing I could think about was the fact that this miniature shorty had turned my fucking life upside down in a matter of months. She was all I fucking thought about outside of my family and getting money and I hated that shit. Her being consumed me and that shit was irritating to say the fucking least. I was hoping that tonight I could get her off of my mind though.

"Tatiana has been holding out on a nigga, so I think I may sample what they have to offer here tonight." Brevin chuckled before sipping his drink.

I bit down on my lip and looked off for a second, allowing Groove and Merce to reply to him. I could no longer care about how he treated Tatiana. That was his bitch and since she liked how he acted I loved it. I was off her, so if he wanted to fuck other bitches raw and have outside babies on her, more power to them both. I chuckled angrily at my thoughts as I threw back my glass of bourbon and refilled it right after.

"Tef, you said your brother was getting out soon?" Brevin looked to me.

Ever since we got back in cahoots I guess, he'd been trying to be my best buddy. I wasn't sure if he was scared of me, or if he genuinely felt bad about what he'd done to Tatiana and didn't fault me for stepping in. Whatever his reasoning was, I wasn't about to be his real friend. Yeah Tatiana was no longer on the menu for me, but I still salivated at the thought of taking over his empire.

"Yeah, he's getting out in some months." I shrugged it off.

I wanted my brother out of jail because I didn't like him being locked away, however I wasn't ready for him to be back in my life. He caused too many damn problems when he was around, which is why for the last five years he's been locked up. At times, I felt it was best but then again he was my blood and I didn't like the fact that he was gone.

"You think he's gonna be looking for work or what?" Brevin questioned me further.

"Man that nigga Torrey does his own thing. He ain't the type to really work for niggas and shit you know," Groove said, referring to my brother.

Brevin just nodded slowly before sipping his drink and eyeing this one thick bitch approaching our table. She was sexy ass hell. Her skin was a smooth vanilla, her lips were plump, and her hair was down her back. I ain't know if the shit was real but it looked real and that was all I cared about. As long as it didn't look like it could be snatched off with a slight tug, or like something would crawl up out, I was fine.

"Hey fellas." She smiled, leaning over the rope a bit.

"What's good, baby?" Brevin licked his lips.

I looked to Merce and saw he was texting away like always when he wasn't around Jadynn. He swore he wasn't only texting her, but I didn't believe him. I liked her for him though because she was down to earth, unlike Savannah's bougie ass.

"Nothing much, what's up with you?" She turned to look me dead in the eyes.

"Chilling." I nodded.

"Are you half Asian? That shit is so sexy."

"Yeah, Vietnamese," I replied, grinning as she blushed.

"Aye, how the fuck you gonna come up in my fucking VIP and address another nigga when you saw me eyeing you! Do you know who the fuck I am?" Brevin barked, stumbling a little as he rose to his feet.

"Chill Brevin!" Groove shouted.

"Nah, this bitch needs to learn to respect the fucking king of Ohio!"

"My bad Brevin, I didn't even know you were feeling me," she replied in a fearful tone. I knew she was lying and only saying what he wanted to hear. It was obvious that he wanted her from the moment she started this way and she knew that.

"Well I am." He calmed down, approaching her. Her body was tense, proving me right about her being afraid. "Come on," he gripped her arm and walked her to the back. She looked over her shoulder at me for a second, with a glum expression.

I couldn't save every woman this nigga came in contact with.

After Brevin fucked her, he came back out and we chilled for a little longer, getting lap dances here and there and just kicking it with some of these fine ass strippers. I usually would have taken one home, but this afternoon was still fresh on my mind. I could still hear the pain in Tatiana's voice as she yelled at Brevin like she loved him.

The four of us headed back to Brevin's and went our separate ways once inside. Groove decided to stay in the guest room since it was so late and he was kind of tipsy. *Good luck explaining that to Cecily*, I thought.

I got into my huge ass bedroom and immediately undressed for a shower. After I finished I brushed my teeth and downed a bottle of room temperature water. After reading a couple texts from some bitches I used to fuck with when I lived here, my baby brother Thomas since he was in a different time zone, and some from an angry Kayla, I placed my phone on the nightstand so I could go to sleep.

As soon as I started to doze off, I felt someone climbing into my bed. When I turned over, I saw Tatiana's ass there, staring at me. She had on some little silk nightgown. The breast area was too big, but she still looked good in it. She looked good in everything she wore.

"You love me?" she quizzed out of nowhere. It was dark but like always her beauty stood out.

"Tati, get out of my bed and go be with your nigga. Make sure he's not about to go fuck somebody else and get them pregnant."

"You are my nigga."

"Nah, I'm really not." I chuckled and turned my back to her. There was a moment of silence and then she dipped under the covers. I felt her small soft hands on my dick, before she covered it with her mouth. "Tatiana, come on man, mmm," I whispered as she deep throated my dick like a porn star.

I threw the covers off so that I could watch her and damn. Seeing her suck me up nastily like that was the shit. I massaged her curly brown hair, as her sexy lips glided up and down my shaft, stopping to suck on the head every now and again. Her hands were so damn soft, so when she reached to play with my balls it intensified the feeling greatly. She sped up her slurps and sucks, getting my dick wet as hell with her saliva. Before I knew it, I was hitting her tonsils and spilling my seeds. She took it down and then instantly mounted me.

"I love you too Tre'Wayne German," she spoke lowly as she made her way down my dick, biting on her lip. Her pussy was so tight and wet, and it seemed to stay that way.

"Shit. Take your gown off." I pushed it upward and gripped her sexy thighs and ass once she caught it. I loved her legs, especially her thighs.

"It's not much to look at," she giggled before pulling it past her head and tossing it.

"I told you I love your body," I replied as I began moving her up and down on my dick. She hadn't quite adjusted to my size yet, but the feeling was unexplainable for me. "Who do you belong to, Tatiana?"

"You," she whimpered, pressing her little hand into my abs as I bounced her slowly on my dick. She came and tossed her head back to wind her hips a little.

I flipped her onto her back, pinned her hands behind her head, and sucked her nipples hungrily while slamming into her. I didn't care who heard us. Gripping her neck, I kissed her nastily as I beat it up with precision, not missing a beat. You could literally hear how wet she was, probably all the way in Rhode Island. I was making my mark on this pussy, so she'd never forget me.

Once she released her juices again, I slid out of her and put her on all fours. I spread her legs and then dipped down to eat her pussy from behind. She was sniveling and whimpering, as I grasped her ass cheeks to hold them apart while devouring her.

"Teeeffffffff," she cried, scraping her nails against the Egyptian cotton sheets.

I continued sucking her clit like it was going out of style, making her cum so hard that her body quivered violently. Sliding back in, I grabbed the back of her neck, pounded her feverishly, yanking another orgasm out of her. By this time, she was wetter than fucking water and clenching my dick like a muthafucka.

"Oh, fuck!" I hollered uncontrollably as I pummeled her middle. I shot off inside of her only a few moments later. "You're mine Tati and don't fucking forget it." I brought her back into my chest to whisper into her ear. My dick was still sitting inside.

"I never have," she panted, chest rising and falling rapidly.

"I got your back baby and you got mine, right?" I questioned and she nodded.

I craned my neck around and slid my tongue into her mouth.

Just that easily she'd improved my mood. Now all I was focused on was getting Brevin's ass out of the way.

CHAPTER NINE

Tatiana

$\mathcal{I}$ was lying on my back trying to think of a way to get Brevin to stop touching me. I hadn't been giving him sex, and I knew he was getting tired of that. He was sleeping with other women so I wasn't quite sure why he still wanted to fuck me, but he did.

Currently his hands were roaming all over my body as he kissed on my neck and collarbone. I was fighting the urge to vomit every time he touched me, because I was genuinely disgusted. I hated him at this point and wasn't sure why I'd even agreed to marry him or make a family with him. The only man that I wanted to be with was Tre'Wayne German or Teflon, as you know him.

"Brevin, I'm not feeling well, maybe later," I nudged him. I truthfully wasn't feeling well and wasn't in the mood to have sex either.

"Come on Tati! Fuck!" he growled, slamming the side of his fist into the area of the bed next to us.

"I had a lot of bleeding in the middle of the night Brevin, let me get up and bathe and stuff. Maybe later tonight I will feel better," I whined, caressing the side of his handsome face.

"You better hope I even come home tonight!" he spat, rolling off me. "You know how many bitches are begging to be in my bed, Tatiana? Yet I'm here sweating you and shit. And at least they have way more ass and titties."

Brevin always insulted my physical when he was upset. It used to kill me when he did that and actually make me cry. Several times, I'd looked up getting breast implants, but I'd never gotten around to it. That's why it took me so long to believe Teflon actually liked the way I looked. But I could see it in his eyes when he gazed at my naked frame that he meant the words he spoke to me.

"Okay Brevin," was all I said as I sat up and swung my feet off the side of the bed. As soon as I stood up, he was in my face, hugging me.

"I didn't mean that, Tatiana."

He gripped my body tightly and began kissing my face, neck, and collarbone again. He was being so rough, and I hated when he did that because it hurt. He was stronger than he realized.

"Move, Brevin. You're hurting me."

He sucked his teeth and pulled away, storming out. I didn't know where he was going, but I was feeling too ill to care.

I went into the bathroom to brush my teeth and then hop into the shower. Once I was finished, I slipped on a short black tube dress and some panties after spreading lotion all over my body. I wore perfume sometimes, but my body butter was a nice scent, and strong enough to be used instead of a perfume.

I went to the drugstore and once I returned I darted up the stairs and went into the bathroom. I retrieved the pregnancy tests from the paper bag and just stared at them for a second.

I'd been pregnant two times before, so I knew the symptoms and I had them. I had no idea what Teflon would think about us having a baby, but an abortion was not an option. Losing two children had made me desperate in a sense to become a mother and at this point, I didn't really care if the father was around.

"Here we go," I sighed, pulling my underwear down and peeing on the stick. I peed on the other one as well to make sure, and then set them on a paper towel before washing my hands.

I left out of the bathroom and sat on the edge of the bed to keep my mind off the test while the few minutes needed passed. As I text Jadynn, and Groove's girlfriend Cecily, Brevin burst into the room. He stared me down for a few, and then leaned down to peck me gently.

"I'm sorry about earlier, I'm just dealing with some shit."

"I know." I nodded with a half smile.

He blew out hot air as he removed his hoodie, and then headed towards the bathroom in my room. It didn't dawn on me that I had my tests in there until he slammed the door closed. I hopped up to rush over, not even sure of what I'd planned to say, and by the time I got there he'd snatched the door open, wearing the angriest expression I'd ever seen on him. Looking down, I spotted the tests clutched tightly in his hands.

"How the fuck are you pregnant Tatiana when I ain't been fucking you huh?" he stepped out of the bathroom towards me, and pulled his gun out, removing the safety.

Join the mailing list to get a notification when Shvonne Latrice has another release!

Text SHVONNE to 66866 to join!

Join my reading group SHVONNE LATRICE READING GROUP on Facebook!